"Who is it you don't trust— yourself or me?" he asked cruelly.

"That isn't fair, Darren."

"Well, are you being fair to me? You know you aren't. It's true that I promised I wouldn't push our relationship further than you wanted it to go, but don't you suppose *I* know how you feel when I kiss you? You want me as much as I want you, and you've kept me dallying for six months. I'm tired of it!"

Ginger faced him bravely. "I'll admit it, I do desire you, but I'll never accept you on your terms."

"So you *do* have a price tag! What is it—a wedding ring? You don't want the other jewelry I buy you, but I suppose you'd gladly take a wedding ring," he said nastily.

"Why, Darren, I wouldn't marry you!"

His surprise couldn't have been greater.

Dear Reader,

The Cherish Romance_{TM} you are about to read is a special kind of romance written with you in mind. It combines the thrill of newfound romance and the inspiration of a shared faith. By combining the two, we offer you an alternative to promiscuity and superficial relationships. Now you can read a romantic novel—with the romance left intact.

Cherish Romances_{TM} will introduce you to exciting places and to men and women very much involved in today's fast-paced world, yet searching for romance and love with commitment—for someone to cherish and be cherished by. You will enjoy sharing their experiences. Most of all you will be uplifted by a romance that involves much more than physical attraction.

Welcome to the world of Cherish Romance_{TM}—a special kind of place with a special kind of love.

Etta Wilson

Etta Wilson, Editor

A Change of Heart

Irene Brand

Cherish
Romances

Thomas Nelson Publishers • Nashville • Camden • New York

Published in Nashville, Tennessee, by Thomas Nelson, Inc. and distributed in Canada by Lawson Falle, Ltd., Cambridge, Ontario.

Printed in the United States of America.

Scripture references in this book are taken from the King James Version of the Bible.

All of the characters in this book are fictitious. Any resemblance to actual persons, living or dead, is purely coincidental.

ISBN 0-8407-7352-8

For my husband
Rod

Chapter One

The car engine had sputtered and completely stopped by the time Ginger Wilson glided to a halt under a huge cottonwood tree beside the road. Having owned the green Volkswagen only two weeks, the red-haired young woman didn't have the least idea what was wrong with it. Nevertheless, Ginger got out of the car, lifted the hood, and peered expectantly at the engine—an action which didn't help at all.

It was late afternoon, and Ginger was stranded in an isolated section of rural Nebraska. After checking the road map, she knew she was still about seventy-five miles from Lincoln, her destination. Thinking that there must be a farmstead somewhere close, she was gazing across the late winter landscape in search of help when a white streak appeared on the highway behind her. The streak soon materialized into a white Cadillac, which slowed and drew to a halt beside her.

The electric window lowered, and a breath of warm air escaped as the driver leaned toward her. "Having trouble, young lady?" asked a dark-haired man with a mustache.

"I'm afraid so," she answered. "I hadn't noticed any problem at all, and suddenly the engine just died."

The man parked the Cadillac in front of Ginger's car and then came striding toward her. Ginger didn't anticipate much help from him. From his appearance, she judged that he had chauffeurs and mechanics to care for his automobiles. He was immaculately dressed in a dark business suit, and nothing about him indicated he had spent much time tinkering under the hood of a car.

"Let's see what the engine sounds like," he said, as he opened the Volkswagen's door and slid into the driver's seat. "I hate midget cars," he muttered and cursed when he bumped his head on the top of her car. He pushed the seat as far back as it would go, but, even then, wedged in with all of Ginger's belongings, he seemed cramped in the driver's position.

The man tried the starter again and again, but the engine refused to turn over. "I believe you're out of gas. How long has it been since you've bought any?"

Ginger leaned into the car to peer at the gas gauge, and was greeted with the fragrance of potent, masculine cologne when her face almost touched his. "I bought gas in Beaver City this morning. The gauge shows more than a fourth of a tank."

Pushing her aside as he opened the door, he walked to the side of the road and bent to pick up a cottonwood twig. Then he inserted the twig into the tank. "Well, you don't have any gas now. Come on, get in my car, and we'll go get some. There's a little town a few miles down the road."

"No, I'll wait here," Ginger said hurriedly.

He smiled knowingly. "Mama told her little girl never to get in a car with a strange man."

She blushed, embarrassed that he had guessed the reason for her refusal. "It was my grandmother," she said with a slight smile.

6

"A kid like you would be better off with me than out here by yourself," he said as he headed for his car, "but do what you like."

His attitude made Ginger argumentative. "I'm not such a kid. I'm almost twenty-four years old."

He halted his stride, and looked at her appraisingly, as if he were seeing her for the first time. She decided that she probably wasn't making much of an impression, dressed in old jeans and a green knit shirt, her red hair blown in every direction by a strong north wind. However, the man smiled and commented with obvious approval, "I guess you aren't such a little girl at that."

With a roar, the white Cadillac came to life, and the stranger was gone before Ginger could think of a suitable retort. She remembered that she hadn't given him any money to buy the gas, and she doubted that he'd send any help at all.

Thinking of his cocksure attitude, she hoped the assistance would come from some other source so that she could avoid accepting his help. But no one else came along.

Ginger Wilson sat in her car for refuge from the whipping wind, and, in a short time, she saw the white automobile returning. With hardly a glance in her direction, he retrieved a can of gas from the trunk of the Cadillac, and poured the fuel into the Volkswagen's tank.

"Now, try to start it. Pump the accelerator a few times," he ordered. From his tone, Ginger was sure that he was in the habit of giving orders, and she didn't like his air of authority.

With only a few struggles, the little car soon was running smoothly. She reached for her purse and handed him a five dollar bill.

"Forget it! I can afford a couple of gallons of gasoline without stretching my budget," he assured her with an easy smile. "But may I ask where you're going, Miss...?" he hesitated, waiting for her name, but Ginger ignored the hint. He motioned to the interior of the car which was packed to the ceiling with her possessions. "You're obviously moving," he stated.

Ginger was unwilling to tell this handsome stranger anything about herself, although she supposed she did owe him something for his help.

"I'm going to Lincoln to work," she said briefly.

"Does your family live there?"

She shook her head.

"Nebraska's capital city is a big place for a girl to be alone."

Ginger was annoyed that her inexperience was that obvious. "I can look after myself," she assured him. "I have to."

A frown appeared on his face, and his eyes darkened menacingly. "Do you have a home there, or a job?" he persisted.

"I have a place to live, and it won't take me long to find a job," she answered as she fastened her seatbelt. "I must go now. I want to get settled before nighttime. Thank you for helping me."

He took a card from his pocket and started writing on it. "Jobs aren't as plentiful as you might think, but this will help you find some work."

"What kind of work?" she asked suspiciously.

He laughed mirthlessly. "I'm beginning to wonder why I've bothered with you, but I suppose it's my public duty to keep another person off the welfare rolls. We employ about seventy-five people, so there should be a place for you." He tossed the card at her

8

and declared, "That will get you a position." Without another glance at her, he got in the Cadillac and drove away.

The calling card's message was enclosed in a golden triangle. It read: Darren W. Banning, President, Midland Bank, Lincoln, Nebraska. On the back he had written, "Personnel Manager, find a position for this young lady. DB."

Ginger started to tear the card in two, but she dropped it in her purse instead. Even so, she would *starve* before she'd accept any more favors from Mr. Darren Banning!

But after three weeks of unsuccessful job hunting, and with the real possibility of starving looming closer, Ginger retrieved the card. If it was a ticket to a job, did she have any choice? Her grandmother's old adage came to mind: "Pride goeth before destruction." Still, she delayed another week before she decided at least to make contact with the bank.

Ginger dressed carefully in a navy blue linen shirtdress with a double collar and cuffs of blue and white. As a final accent, she wore her single strand of pearls in the open V-neck of the dress and added plain pearl earrings.

The navy blue gave a bluish hue to her gray eyes and enhanced her ginger-colored hair. She had to admit that she was a little curious to see Darren Banning again, but, as she entered the door of the Midland Bank, she doubted that it was the place for her.

The front of the three-story buff brick structure was made almost entirely of glass. Subdued organ music wafted throughout the lobby, and a sense of peace and quiet prevailed even though there was a crowd of patrons and employees. Ginger had a momentary feeling of entering a cathedral, but that quickly gave way to the impression of an art gallery as she moved farther inside.

The designers had commemorated the western heritage of the region in the decor. Behind the tellers' windows was an immense mural depicting a homestead scene. The head of mounted elk and buffalo reposed over many of the office doors. Long brass chandeliers hung from the two-story ceiling, and a giant Indian chief mosaic looked over the lobby from a wall behind the silent escalator.

"This is no place for a country girl like me," Ginger muttered, knowing, even as she said it, that she would enjoy working in such a fabulous setting. She spotted the personnel manager's desk not far from where she stood. She walked slowly across the deep green plush carpeted floor, and waited quietly by the desk until the man looked up. Then, without a word, she handed him the card.

"Oh, yes," he said smilingly. "Mr. Banning said you would be in." Annoyed by what she considered another example of Banning's smugness, Ginger wished she hadn't come; but she had, so she sat down and filled out the application form. In fifteen minutes, she had a position as a bank teller!

Ginger worked at the bank for nearly a month before she saw Darren Banning again, but she had *heard much* about him by then. He was a favorite subject of conversation in the lounge; and, if all comments were to be accepted, Darren Banning was a godlike being, with a few devilish traits to add spice to his character. Ginger got the impression that many of the women gladly would have changed places with his personal secretary—and current flame—Maureen Rowley, who ruled like a queen in the reception room outside his office.

Ginger watched every day for the bank president to appear. Finally she quizzed Tina Alleman, the teller who worked beside her.

"Oh, Mr. Banning has various interests," Tina replied. "He's probably down in Texas drilling an oil well, or up in the Sand Hills playing around on his ranch. He isn't here very much, but he'll show up one of these days."

If she thought that her presence at the bank would cause much of a reaction from Darren, she was due for a disappointment. When he came at last, he merely smiled at her, and gave her an ironic salute as he strode across the lobby. She was acutely aware of him, however, for his personality transformed the bank into an exciting environment. He seemed to be everywhere at once as he greeted customers, conferred with the bank officers, and chatted with employees. His resonant voice and vibrant laugh resounded throughout the building.

On the second day after his return, Ginger arrived at work to find a florist's box lying on her counter. Curious, she opened the box and found an orchid corsage! Her fingers trembled as she read the card: "Welcome to Midland Bank, *Miss Wilson*. DB." He had underlined her name, apparently to remind her that he'd learned the name anyway.

She closed the box hurriedly, but Tina already had seen it. "Who's it from?" she asked, and took the card from Ginger's hand. Tina's face registered amazement. "Well! Well! Well!" she said with a knowing smile.

Ginger felt her face flushing. "Is this a usual procedure?" she asked hopefully. "Does he send corsages to all new employees?"

"I've been here for nine years, and you're the first person I've known to get a welcoming gift." Tina hesitated a bit, and then she added, "I think I'd better have a talk with you."

Darren still didn't stop to speak, but, once that day, when he passed by, he did look pointedly at her shoulder, to see if she were wearing the corsage. She was not—it remained in the box all day. Ginger tried to ignore him, but a mental image of his dark hair and handsome face, highlighted by smooth, mustached lips, was with her whether he was in the room or not.

When the day's work ended, Tina walked with Ginger to the parking lot. "How about giving me a ride for a few blocks? My car is in the garage, and I'm on foot today."

"Sure," Ginger said, although she wondered how Tina's large frame would fit in the green Volkswagen. Tina was tall and stocky, with a definite roll of fat around the waist, but she was still pretty, and her pleasing personality was more obvious than her size.

Downtown Lincoln was always teeming with people at five o'clock, when university students and shoppers mingled with workers eager to get home after a day's work. Ginger had to wait several minutes before she could pull out on busy O Street.

When they stopped at a red light, Tina asked, "How did you meet Darren Banning?"

Ginger was reluctant to tell her, but briefly explained the encounter with Darren on the road.

Tina laughed. "Handsome gentleman rescues maiden in distress—a regular storybook romance." She laughed again. "When I saw you coming to work with that mass of red hair tumbling over your shoulders, and in those stylish clothes you wear, I just knew that you were Maureen Rowley's replacement! I had

12

the feeling he was getting tired of her."

"Oh, no!" Ginger protested. "I don't have any interest in him."

"That's not the point. He's interested in you, and you can bet on that."

"I'm sure you're wrong. Besides, I came up here to go to school, and I'm working to pay my way through the university. Going to school at night and working all day won't give me any time for romance. He'll soon learn that."

They were stalled in traffic again, and Tina twisted in the cramped seat and looked at Ginger. "You're a mystery to me, kid. Where'd you come from? How can you afford to wear such charming outfits?" She indicated Ginger's simple rust dress, with an attached, side-draped paisley scarf.

Ginger smiled at her friend. "There's nothing mysterious about me. I lived with my grandmother on the farm in southwestern Nebraska until I graduated from high school. Then I spent a year in Kansas City with my mother who was a buyer for a large dress firm. Since I had a flair for sewing, Mother enrolled me in a special school to train as a fashion designer. I won several awards for making and designing my own clothes. So most of these dresses I have I've patterned after models in fashion magazines." She paused for a moment. "There, you have the story of my life."

Tina whistled in amazement. "With a background like that, what are you doing here?"

"A couple of things happened to make me leave KC. My mother remarried and moved with her husband to the Middle East. He's in the oil business. I didn't want my stepfather to finance my education. About that time, my grandmother became ill, and I went back to the farm to care for her. When she died a few months ago, she left all of her property to me. I couldn't envision myself running a farm, so I rented the property, took the money she had, bought a mobile home and this car, and here I am."

"Are you going to study fashion designing here?"

"No. I liked the designing work itself, but I was appalled by the lifestyle of the people in the fashion business. Everyone seemed determined to strike it rich—one way or another."

Tina laughed. "You're working at the wrong place if you want to escape materialism."

"Maybe, but I couldn't find a job elsewhere, and I have to work to provide my needs until I achieve my real goal. I want to help the underprivileged, so I'm enrolled in the Special Education program at the university."

Tina was never passive in her reactions, and she whistled again. "I can see you're a gal who knows what she wants in life, and more power to you!"

They were passing the towering state capitol which dominated Lincoln's skyline, and Tina said, "Pull in at the next corner. I live down the street." But when Ginger turned off the ignition, Tina made no move to get out of the car.

"It's none of my business, Ginger, but I think you should know a little about Mr. Banning, in case he does make a play for you. He's a good employer most of the time, but he's got a hard streak in him. That's why I said you'd come to the wrong place to escape materialism. He's determined to be superior in everything he does." Ginger's pulse quickened as Tina told her things which she would rather not have heard. "He came to the bank a few years back, and he wasn't content with owning the controlling interest. He continued to buy all the stock he could so that he almost

14

owns the whole corporation now. I know this because my grandfather is one of the stockholders, and Banning has been trying to buy his shares. He must have millions of dollars, but he's determined to make more and more. If someone makes a bad investment at the bank sometimes, he raises the devil."

Ginger felt impelled to defend him. "Of course, it's only natural that he would want his organization to be successful."

"Maybe, but he has a tendency to go overboard. And he's rather mysterious, too. None of us knows anything about his past before he came here, and, occasionally, when he comes back from one of his long absences, he looks burdened, as if the weight of the world were on his shoulders." Tina opened the door and got out. "I've said all I'm going to, but I wanted you to know there's more to Darren Banning than meets the eye."

After leaving Tina, Ginger guided her car to Interstate 80 and drove a few miles west of Lincoln to the trailer park where her new mobile home was situated. Although she didn't like driving to and from work in the city, she wanted the peace of the countryside when day's end came. Even with fifty mobile homes around her, she still could enjoy a bit of rural Nebraska. Her home was on the periphery of the park, and, from her kitchen window, she looked westward over a broad expanse of farmland.

Ginger tried to forget Tina's remarks, but she couldn't put them out of her mind. Men had played a minor role in Ginger's life up until now. Living on a farm and attending small schools hadn't prepared Ginger to cope with men like Darren Banning—and this was one time when Ginger wished her grandmother hadn't been so protective and conservative.

The next morning, soon after the bank opened for business, Darren came from his office, accompanied by Maureen Rowley, and they left the building together. They were a stunning couple! The sight of Maureen's full-bosomed, tall figure, encased in a pink knit suit, dampened Ginger's spirits. She had to admit that the woman was beautiful, although Ginger found it difficult to like her. Of all the main-floor employees at the bank, Ginger was least acquainted with Maureen, who held herself aloof from the rest of the employees.

During their lunch break, Tina told Ginger, "The Big Boss has gone to Denver for a banking convention."

"Did Maureen go with him?" Ginger found herself asking.

Tina raised a mug of coffee to her lips, and her eyes were expressive. "Always! You don't think he keeps her around just for decoration, do you?"

"Hasn't Mr. Banning ever been married?" Ginger inquired.

"Not in the years I've known him. Anytime one of his so-called 'personal secretaries' gets into her head that she wants to become Mrs. Darren Banning, she leaves in a hurry! Maureen is the *fifth* secretary he's had since he came here." She shook her head. "No, he definitely isn't the marrying type, and," Tina added, "don't say I didn't warn you."

Tina's assessment of Darren only served to enforce Ginger's obsession with him. She had put other men out of her mind easily enough, but Darren appealed to her in a manner that she didn't understand. Why did her hands tremble when she heard his voice? Why did the sight of his large frame striding across a room leave her breathless? Such emotions were new to her, and she wasn't sure she had the wisdom to deal with them.

After a sleepless night of frustration, and realizing that her interest in Darren might interfere with her other plans, Ginger recommitted her future to God's guidance. Her grandmother's views may have been old-fashioned, but the dear woman's biblical teachings of honesty, decency, morality, and kindness remained the same from generation to generation. Ginger Wilson would need to remember that if she had any more contact with Darren.

She made up her mind to avoid him as much as possible, but, each day, she dressed with particular care, and when she entered the bank her first glance was to see if his office was occupied.

It remained empty all week.

Chapter Two

Darren and Maureen were back on Monday morning, and all week the bank responded to Darren's bustling vitality. Staff and board meetings were held in his office. He conferred with individual officers. The place was full and vibrant.

If Darren ever glanced her way, Ginger didn't see it, but she was as conscious of his presence or absence as the earth is sensitive to the rays of the sun. Although she needed the job and liked working at the Midland Bank, she was miserable now. She began to wish Darren would leave on one of his long absences, so she could settle down to normal living again.

It was about closing time on Friday when she answered the phone at her teller's station and heard Darren's voice on the line. "Miss Wilson, will you step into my office before you leave for the day?" he requested.

She had to swallow twice before she answered, and, even then, her voice sounded strained. "I'll be in soon." She moved as though she were in a trance as she carried her money box to the vault for night deposit. Her legs were so shaky that she could hardly walk the short distance to his office.

Darren was talking on the phone when she entered, and he motioned for her to sit down. While he continued the conversation, she surveyed his office domain. The room was huge, with the western theme evident throughout. The thick turquoise carpet was decorated with various cattle brands. The room's furnishings, including the spacious desk, were of rustic pine. Paintings of prairie scenes hung on the walls, and a bronze bust of the Indian chief, Sitting Bull, stood on a pedestal behind Darren's desk. A mirror framed in a golden triangle was near the door to Maureen's office.

After he hung up the phone, Darren looked at Ginger for a long while. She smiled timidly at him, but finally lowered her eyes from his unfriendly gaze.

"Don't you like orchids, Miss Wilson?" he said at last.

She glanced shyly at him. "They're all right, I guess. I'd never had one before." She spoke with an effort, and she hoped that he hadn't detected the tremor in her voice.

"Well, surely you know enough about corsages to understand they're supposed to be *worn*. I expected you to wear the one I sent you."

Why could he always make her feel like she was five years old again? Ginger wondered. Ginger knew she was acting like a reprimanded child, but the man intimidated her. "Tina Alleman said you hadn't sent any other new employee a gift, and I was embarrassed to wear it."

"Tina talks too much." That comment didn't seem to warrant an answer, and Ginger remained silent. Darren then demanded, "What did you do with the corsage?"

"It's at home in the refrigerator." She added, "I'm

sorry I annoyed you, because I do appreciate getting the job here."

Still without smiling, he said, "I'll show I've forgiven you by taking you to dinner tonight. I think you'll like the food at the Sailmaker. Will six o'clock be convenient?"

Ginger's heart did a little flip-flop, but she nonetheless resented his gall in assuming that all he had to do was to ask, and she'd be ready to go. "That's very thoughtful of you, Mr. Banning, but I have other plans tonight."

He looked surprised, and Ginger guessed that he wasn't used to any woman refusing him. It would do him good to be rejected once in a while, she reasoned.

"I should have suspected that," he admitted. "What about tomorrow evening?"

"No, I'm busy then, too. Thank you, but, if you'll excuse me, I'll get back to work." She smiled warmly, and left him.

She was sure that Darren had thought she was lying about her appointment, but she wasn't. Her evening had been planned several weeks ago.

Arriving at the mobile home park, Ginger went first to the trailer of her next-door neighbors, Sally and Roger Stone. They had befriended Ginger as soon as she had moved beside them. The Stones had invited her to their church, and Ginger had enjoyed the worship and fellowship at the small church a mile from the park.

Ginger was also fond of Sally's brother, Ken Grady. He was a part-time student at the university, and he sometimes drove Ginger to her classes. Tonight, Ken and his parents had invited several friends from church out to their farm to cook steaks and go for a hayride afterward. Ginger was looking forward to the evening at the Grady farm, hoping that the fellowship of her friends would erase the turmoil she had experienced since her chance meeting with Darren Banning.

"Hi!" Sally greeted Ginger as she opened the door, holding one-year-old Patrick in her arms. Sally always brightened Ginger's day. "I thought you were going to be late. As soon as Roger gets dressed, we're going on out to help Mother. Ken had to make a quick trip into town for farm supplies, but he'll come back and pick you up in about an hour."

"Good. That will give me time to make the potato salad," Ginger said as she hurried over to her home.

Soon she had made enough salad to fill a large plastic bowl, and there was still enough time left to shower and change into some fresh clothes.

Ginger decided to wear knee socks and desert boots with her jeans and green flannel shirt. It was sure to be cool before the evening was over. Just as she was pulling on a hooded sweatshirt, the doorbell rang. Ken was early.

"Just a minute," she called. She turned off the bedroom light and hurried into the living room.

Darren Banning, not Ken, was standing at the door! Behind him in the driveway was the white Cadillac which seemed almost as long as her trailer.

"Why, Mr. Banning!" she cried in surprise. "How did you know where I lived?"

He smiled pleasantly. "Midland Bank does record the addresses of its employees, Miss Wilson. A few discreet inquiries brought me right to your door."

"I would invite you in, but I'm getting ready to go out."

"Have you changed your mind about having dinner with me?"

21

His persistence both irritated and pleased her. Whatever his reason, she liked having him seek her company.

"I really do have plans for the evening. Did you think I was lying?"

He smiled knowingly. "I thought you might want to be persuaded."

She frowned. "If you think I lie, you must have a high opinion of me!"

Before Darren could reply, Ken Grady's dilapidated farm truck pulled in behind the sleek Cadillac. As he unwound his lanky sandy-haired frame from the truck cab, it was obvious he had been to the feed store.

Ginger opened the door and stepped out under the awning as Ken approached. He looked questioningly from Ginger to Darren.

"Mr. Banning, this is my friend, Ken Grady. Ken, Darren Banning is the president of Midland Bank."

Ken looked quickly at his dusty hands, and wiped the right hand on his jeans before extending it to Darren. "I'm pleased to meet you, Mr. Banning." Darren nodded his head, but said nothing. Ken turned to Ginger. "Are you ready? I can come back later if you're busy."

"No, no," Ginger assured him. "I'm ready. Mr. Banning had just stopped by. He knew that I had plans for the evening. Wait until I get my salad and lock the house."

While she was inside, Ginger heard Ken saying, "Why don't you come along with us, Mr. Banning? We're having supper at our house, and we're going on a hayride later. You're surely welcome."

"No, thank you, Ken. I've always heard that three is a crowd."

Ken laughed. "Oh, Ginger and I won't be alone.

There'll be about fifteen of us!"

"I'll pass up the invitation this time. Thanks." Ginger couldn't imagine anyone who would be more out of place on a hayride than Darren Banning!

He was still there when she came out. Since his Cadillac was wedged in by Ken's pickup and her Volkswagen, he couldn't very well leave until one of them moved.

"I hope you understand, Mr. Banning," she said. He just stood by his automobile and watched them leave. His face was expressionless—except for a sadness in his eyes that Ginger hadn't detected before.

While Ken was turning the truck, he said, "Ginger, I've always thought you were an intelligent girl until now."

"What do you mean?" she asked in surprise.

"Although I don't know exactly what was going on here tonight, I can't imagine why anyone would go someplace with me in this old truck, when you obviously had a chance to go out with that?" He motioned toward Darren in all his finery.

Ginger suppressed a giggle. Darren did make quite an imposing picture standing beside the big car, which had golden triangles emblazoned on both front doors. He was wearing a vested linen suit of desert tan, and a golden triangle fastener secured the braided tie to the neck of his brown shirt. No doubt about it—Ken was a less dynamic figure. But Ginger remembered another of her grandmother's sayings, "Handsome is as handsome does," an adage which she was certain applied in this case.

When she waved good-bye, he raised his hand in an ironic salute. Darren needed to be jolted from his arrogant attitude, but she couldn't help wondering what it would be like to spend an evening with him. She supposed that she had lost the chance to find out.

Ginger had a good time with her friends, but, all evening, her thoughts were never far from the handsome banker with the mustache.

She would have liked the luxury of sleeping late the next morning, but Saturday was Ginger's busiest day. She had some sewing to do and a term paper to type.

Ginger hurried through her weekly house-cleaning. The newness of her mobile home made cleaning it a pleasure. The living room, kitchen, and dining area comprised more than half of the dwelling. A wooden bar and three stools divided the living room from the kitchen. Ginger's typewriter and a portable black-and-white television were on the bar. A small walnut table and four chairs were in front of the bay window. She had furnished her home with items from her grandmother's house, and she enjoyed this bond with her past. A narrow hall led from the kitchen to one large bedroom, a bathroom, and the small utility area.

Before she finished, a neighbor from across the street came for a visit, and she stayed for more than an hour. Mrs. Gainer was an elderly woman, who had recently been widowed and needed companionship. Ginger tried to be patient with her, but the visit did delay her work. It was mid-afternoon before she finished typing the term paper.

It was almost dusk when she finally started to sew. Ginger laid the various pieces of material around the living room. Because she was sitting with her back to the door and operating the machine, she didn't hear a sound until the doorbell rang. Darren Banning was at the door again! She had been thinking about him all day, and now it was as if he had stepped out of her thoughts.

24

She opened the door, and the ceiling of her mobile home seemed to shrink when he stepped in. With a smile, he said, "If at first you don't succeed, try again. I find it hard to compete with a handsome youth who drives a beatup truck, but I come bearing gifts anyway." He handed her a long florist's box.

Ginger laid the box on the bar and moved some fabric from her grandmother's rocker to give him a place to sit down. She opened the box and found a dozen red roses! She was utterly speechless as she got a white vase and arranged the flowers in it.

Her fingers shook as she removed the last of the scented flowers from the box. What did he mean by all of this attention? Now that he had invaded the privacy of her home, no place would offer respite from his forceful personality. At the bank, his presence was everywhere. Now, could she ever enter her living room without seeing him sitting, debonair and handsome, in that chair?

"Thank you," she finally said, as she perched on one of the bar stools.

He looked around the littered room. "I see you're busy as you said. What are you doing?"

"I'm making two dresses."

He raised his eyebrows and one of them arched in a most fascinating manner. *Even his eyebrows seem to form triangles*, Ginger thought.

"You make your own clothes?" he asked in amazement.

"Most of them."

"That surprises me. You always look so chic. I assumed you spent all of your money on clothes."

Ginger merely shook her head, and smiled slightly.

"I hoped you could have dinner with me tonight," he said.

Ginger laughed at the man's persistence. "Saturday is the only time I have to get any work done here at home, Mr. Banning. I told you that. I'm not going anyplace tonight, but it will be late before I finish my sewing. I'm sure you can find another companion for the evening." She wanted to ask him if Maureen was busy, but she held her tongue.

He answered coldly, "It isn't that I can't find company. I'm asking you, but you're the busiest person I've encountered in months." He took a datebook from his pocket. "Let's see, this is the latter part of April." He flipped a few pages. "I wonder if you could spare me an hour or two of your time during September." Now he was adding sarcasm to his arrogance.

"If you're so dead-set on my company," Ginger said, "we won't have to wait that long. How about tomorrow afternoon? I never work on Sundays. Would that suit you?"

He lowered his head, and Ginger couldn't tell from his expression if he were pleased or not. "That sounds fine. When can I meet you?"

"I'll be home from church about noon."

He stood to leave. "Then I'll leave you to your sewing." Ginger stood for a long time at the door after he had exited and was out of sight. What would she do tomorrow?

The white Cadillac wasn't there when she returned from church the next day. With a let-down feeling, Ginger wondered if he had changed his mind. Soon, however, the doorbell rang.

Darren was all smiles as he escorted her to the car, but her palms were wet, and her voice trembled as she conversed with him.

He was dressed casually, in an open-necked plaid

shirt, white soft suede jacket, and tan trousers. Her pink linen dress with white sweater jacket must have met his approval, for he gazed at her admiringly. "You look lovely today. Is that the dress you were making yesterday?"

"Yes. I finished it about midnight."

"I wouldn't have thought you could wear pink with your hair, but it's most becoming." To her dismay, Ginger felt her face flushing, and she wished she could display an air of sophistication.

She sat far to the right side of the car. The interior was just as impressive as the exterior, with its white velour upholstery and white shag carpeting.

As big as the car was, Ginger felt smothered by Darren's presence. As he started the engine, he said smilingly, "Since you have such a busy schedule, I'll need to know how much of your time I'm allowed today."

She wasn't used to this side of the dynamic Mr. Banning, and she wondered if he were teasing her. Without looking at him, she answered, "I'm free for the afternoon, but I want to be home in time for church tonight."

The big car purred into life. "Then the next question. Are you already hungry?"

"No, not at all," she said truthfully. She doubted that she would be able to eat a bite in his presence anyway, for her stomach felt as if it were tied in knots.

"Then I'd like to take you to Omaha to eat. We can be up there in a little more than an hour. Have you visited any of the restaurants at the Old Market?"

"No, I haven't been to Omaha since a school trip when I was a ninth grader. The Old Market has been developed since then."

He soon put her at ease, and she began to talk freely as they moved along. Before they had arrived in

Omaha, he knew about her grandmother's death, her reason for coming to Lincoln, and her desire to acquire a college degree. She learned very little about him. He wasn't inclined to talk about himself, and she was too wary to ask questions. The luxurious automobile seemed to float along the road, and, when she closed her eyes, Ginger had the sensation of drifting through time and space. The car's FM radio effused soothing, stereo music.

They left Interstate 80 at the last exit before it crossed the Missouri River into Iowa, and drove into Old Market, a restoration of Omaha's wholesale jobbing section of the late 1800s. They walked along streets lined with fruit vendors' stalls, antique shops, used book stores, and sidewalk cafés. Soon they came to a restaurant called Wagons West housed in an ancient brick building. The rooms were decorated with Victorian antiques and a few vintage automobiles.

When the waiter brought the menu, Darren asked, "Will you allow me to order for us?"

She found no fault with his choice. First they visited the salad bar, which was displayed in the bed of an old truck. The rest of the meal—rare roast beef, baked potatoes, creamed asparagus, and hot rolls—was delicious. The dessert course of flaming Baked Alaska caused Ginger's eyes to widen in delight.

She realized that Darren was amused at her naivete, but she didn't care. She was having a good time. Her escort was entertaining, he was polite, and he was handsome. What else could a girl ask? She was enjoying each moment to the fullest; she'd been allotted one day of his precious time, and she knew it would be the last. Tomorrow he would be back to Maureen.

As they finished dessert, Darren reached across the table and covered Ginger's hand with his. She was surprised at the gentleness of his touch and at the sensations that pulsated through her body. She quickly withdrew her hand from his touch.

"Having a good time?" he asked. The expression on his face was one which she hadn't seen before. He seemed more relaxed than usual, and he looked much younger.

"Oh, yes," Ginger answered softly.

"Strangely enough, so am I," he said, almost in wonder. Pushing back his chair, he said, "Had enough?"

"More than enough. You've ruined my diet."

While they waited for the check, he said, "You surely don't have to diet, a little thing like you? How much do you weigh?"

"About a hundred pounds," she told him as they left the table. She couldn't help but notice the sizeable tip that he left. It was enough to have bought her groceries for a week!

As they walked out into the balmy April afternoon, he looked at his watch. "We still have a few hours before you have to be home. Would you like to take the scenic route? We could drive south along the Missouri, then return to Lincoln on the back roads."

"Yes, I'd like that. I'm a country girl, you know. That's the reason I placed my mobile home on the outskirts of town. I don't enjoy the city very much."

"Neither do I. If I did what I wanted, I'd stay at the ranch all of the time."

They were leaving Omaha behind as they drove southward. She glanced sideways and smiled at him. "I thought you *always* did what you wanted," she dared to say. "Why *don't* you stay on the ranch?"

"It's simple! I can't make enough money there. Sometimes I have to dip into my other accounts to keep the ranch going. I play at ranching, but all my other interests are dead serious."

"And making money is that important to you?"

"Making money is a challenge to me, and I like power and the things money can buy."

Ginger became silent, sensing that her values and his were unalterably opposed.

The road they followed paralleled the Missouri River, and occasionally they had a glimpse of the giant stream. When they reached Plattsmouth, where the Platte River flowed into the Missouri, Darren turned the big car westward beside a sign that read, "Canoe Livery, 2 miles."

"Have you ever taken a canoe ride, Miss Wilson?" he inquired.

"No," she said, as much surprised that he seemed in no hurry to return to Lincoln as she was by the question.

"I haven't for a few years, but I don't think I've forgotten the art of canoeing. How about a short trip on the Platte? We shouldn't waste such a summer-like afternoon."

"I'm willing," she said. "It sounds like fun."

They made arrangements to rent the canoe, and, as they walked down to the water, Darren said, "This may not be the best idea I've had. Neither of us is dressed suitably for canoeing."

Ginger laughed nervously as she watched other canoeists leaving the dock. "And I forgot to say that I can't swim!"

"Miss Wilson, someone has neglected your education. You can't swim, you haven't been canoeing, and you hadn't eaten Baked Alaska. I'll have to take you in hand."

Ginger didn't answer, but she warmed with inexplicable emotion. Was he just talking, or did he intend to see her again?

"Anyway, you won't have to swim, we hope. Here's your paddle," he said, handing her an oar.

She took it helplessly. "I don't know what to do with it."

"I'll show you," he assured her, patting her on the arm.

When the attendant put the canoe into the water, Darren held the sides of the boat until Ginger was seated in the stern.

"All set?" he asked with a smile. She nodded uncertainly as he settled himself in the front of the canoe, with his back to her and spoke over his shoulder. "We'll paddle on opposite sides of the canoe. It will probably be more natural for you to paddle on the right side, so I'll take the left. To keep the canoe balanced, be sure you don't wiggle around. Just dip the oar in the water as far as it will reach, like this," he demonstrated.

Ginger moved the paddle slowly, and he encouraged her. "That's it. Just don't be nervous. I can paddle by myself if necessary, so if your arms get tired, let me know."

He motioned for the attendant to loosen the rope holding them, and they moved out across the water as Darren smiled encouragingly over his shoulder. He steered out into the deeper current, and they moved slowly downstream.

Waterfowl scattered at their approach, and a mother duck hustled her ducklings to safety. Boys swimming from one of the numerous sandbars in the river waved at them as Ginger and Darren went by, and they passed several canoes traveling upstream toward the livery.

He looked back at Ginger frequently, and the smile

31

he gave her each time made her more determined to master the canoeing. She wanted to please him.

Once, when he glanced backward, he frowned, and Ginger asked, "What am I doing wrong?"

"It isn't you. I'm watching that canoe behind us. A couple of kids in it are goofing around." When he looked again, he roared, "Watch out, you idiots!"

Ginger turned to see another canoe bearing down upon them. The two boys noticed Ginger and Darren at that same time, but they were already too close, and the canoe struck Ginger's paddle! The wood splintered from her grasp with a jerk, pulling her sideways.

Darren shouted to the boys, "Get away from us," and to Ginger, "Sit still. I can paddle alone."

But the boys had lost control of their canoe after the impact, and the craft careened wildly into the bow of Darren and Ginger's boat, beside Darren. The canoe lurched crazily, hurling Ginger sideways into the river! She screamed as the cold water closed over her head, and she felt as if she were swallowing the whole Platte River. When she came to the surface, spitting and sputtering, Darren was in the water beside her.

He grabbed her arm as she started to sink again. "Hold on to me, Ginger. There's absolutely nothing to worry about. Just keep your arm around my waist, and don't struggle." He started swimming toward shore.

Strangely enough, she never doubted that he would save her. She could feel the powerful muscles moving freely in his back as he exerted all of his strength to carry her extra weight. In a few minutes, he pulled her to safety onto a sandbar, where he collapsed and inhaled deeply until he breathed normally again.

The empty canoe was bobbing downstream, and the canoe carrying the two boys was moving swiftly toward the livery. Darren and Ginger were cut off from shore by another channel of water.

"The next time I ask if you want to go canoeing, say 'no!' We're in a real mess now!" Darren said ruefully, as he pulled off his shoes and dumped water out of them. Ginger wanted to laugh at his appearance—sodden clothes hung limp on his well-formed body, and his dark hair was matted to his head.

Water was dripping from Ginger's long red hair, and she self-consciously pulled the clinging clothes away from her breasts and hips. One of her shoes was gone, and Darren noted its absence at the same time that she did.

"Where's your shoe?" he demanded.

She laughed a little. "Guess!"

"Do I look as bad as you do?" he asked.

She nodded, and both of them burst out laughing in abandonment. Darren recovered first. "Well, it really isn't funny. You could easily have drowned. I'd like to choke those two kids! The least they could have done was to stay and help us."

Looking up and down the river, he continued, "We'll wait a bit to see if anyone comes by who can send some help." He looked at his watch, which, by some miracle, was still running. "It's almost six o'clock, so likely there won't be many more people out tonight."

After awhile, when no one had appeared, he said, "We'll just have to wade ashore. That channel doesn't look like it's too deep, but there could be quicksand in it. This river is treacherous in spots, but we can't stay here all night." He took her hand. "If we step into a deep hole, stay close to me."

With very little swimming, and no more mishaps, they made it to the southern shore of the Platte, where

33

they rested again before starting the walk back to the livery.

Ginger had no choice except to walk barefoot, and their progress was slowed because of that, along with the heavy underbrush of briers and willows through which they had to crawl. Their clothes were soiled and torn beyond repair by the time they arrived at the livery an hour later.

He handed the car keys to her as he prepared to go report on the fate of the canoe. "I don't want to sit on that white upholstery as dirty as I am," Ginger said. "Do you suppose you can get some plastic to cover the seats?"

"Look in the trunk. I keep some blankets back there."

She was sitting on the covered front seat by the time he returned. He leaned over and kissed her lightly on the forehead. "That's the first time I ever kissed a girl whose face tasted like sand," he said with a grimace.

"Well, I've been out with neater-looking men myself," she retorted good-naturedly.

He brushed the damp hair back from her forehead. "I don't suppose you'll ever forget our first date, though," he said, and Ginger looked away. He kept talking as if there would be a next time.

"You were a mighty brave girl. Most females would have screamed and fought. You just held on and acted like getting pulled from the water was an everyday occurrence."

"You said not to worry, and I trusted you."

Seriously, he said, "You *can* trust me. Do you believe it?"

She sensed that he meant more than trusting him to save her from drowning. Her voice was a mere whisper when she answered, "I want to believe it."

He squeezed her hand. "You can." His mood changing suddenly, he said, "Let's head for Lincoln. I'd like to stop for something to eat, but I wouldn't want to eat in any restaurant that would let us in the way we look."

He followed the rural roads, and, despite her wet and grimy condition, Ginger enjoyed the sight of the neat farms, the white farm buildings, and the livestock grazing on the greening pastures. Memories of her grandmother's farm came to mind, and she felt sad at the loss of this person whom she had loved so much.

When they passed the church, lights were on, and music could be heard wafting from the open windows. Darren looked at his watch. "No church for you tonight. I am sorry; I intended to bring you back in time."

"I'm not blaming you." She'd been thinking about something for the past few miles, uncertain whether to mention it or not, but she decided to take the risk. "After all the lunch I ate, I didn't think I'd ever be hungry again, but it seems I am. If you'd like to come in, I can prepare a snack for us."

"That's a good girl! I'm eager to get out of these clothes, but, on the other hand, I don't want to go to the apartment, then come back out to eat. You won't have to go to a great deal of trouble?"

"No, I'm used to preparing meals in a hurry."

Mrs. Gainer was peering out the window when they drove in, and she watched them going into the trailer. Ginger pulled the drapes against inquisitive eyes. "Let me have a few minutes to clean up. Then you can take your turn in the bathroom while I prepare our food."

Ginger sponged off quickly and brushed some of the grime out of her hair. She changed into a wraparound skirt and a royal blue top with cap sleeves, and she slipped into some barefoot sandals.

While Darren was in the bathroom, she made ground beef patties, and put them under the broiler. Fortunately, she had prepared vegetables for salad before she had left for church this morning. She placed two plates on the table, and set out butter, cheese, and crackers.

Darren returned to sit on one of the stools. With elbows anchored on the bar, he watched her. Acutely conscious of his presence, she filled a glass with ice and 7-Up and offered it to him. "Here's a drink to hold you until the meat is ready."

He accepted the glass gratefully. "I see you're a lady of many skills—bank teller, scholar, seamstress, and now a cook."

She smiled at him over her shoulder, the red hair partly concealing her face. "You have quite a few talents yourself—banker, businessman, rancher, swimmer, canoeist..."

He grinned wryly. "I'm not so sure about that last one."

"Do you want coffee or tea? The coffee is instant. I don't drink it myself, but the Stones and Ken like coffee, so I keep it for them."

"Does Ken visit you often?"

Ginger didn't think that that was any of his business, but she didn't say so. "No, not much, but we ride to the university together. Sometimes he comes in for a cup of coffee in the evening when we get home."

He made no comment on that, but answered her previous question. "I'll take coffee. I'm used to instant coffee; it's the only kind I can prepare myself. I'm not much of a cook."

Ginger was surprised to hear him admit that there was something he couldn't do!

Before they started eating, Ginger hesitantly said, "I

always ask God's blessing on the food before I eat."

He placed his hands on the table and answered, "It's your home. Do what you want."

She offered a simple prayer of thanks in a low voice. When she raised her head, Darren said, "Miss Wilson, you continue to amaze me."

Ginger didn't know what he meant by the remark, and she had no intention of asking him. She did note that they were back to "Miss Wilson" again.

She wondered if he would like her rather plain food, but he ate heartily. When she served homemade apple pie with ice cream he praised it.

"This pie is delicious! I'll have to tell Melissa that I've finally found someone who can make better pies than she."

When he noted Ginger's look of curiosity, he added, "Melissa is the housekeeper at the ranch. Her husband, Ike, is my ranch manager."

Thank goodness, Melissa has a husband. At least I won't have any competition from her. As if you are even in the running for his favors! Ginger mentally chided herself.

Darren stood to leave and moved close to her. "What about a good-bye kiss?"

"Oh, no," Ginger backed away until the bar separated them.

Darren laughed gently. "Well, all right!" he said. He held out his hand. "At least we can shake hands to put a seal on the most enjoyable day I've had in a long time, Miss Wilson."

She put her hand in his, and glanced up shyly at him, wondering if he really meant what he said. "I've had a good time, too," she said softly. "Canoe ride and all."

He lifted her open hands to his lips, and they

seemed to burn her skin as his soft mustache brushed across her palm in an intimate caress. After he left, she stood for a long time, her palm pressed to her lips.

Chapter Three

Ginger felt as though her temperature rose several degrees when she first heard Darren's voice in the tellers' area the next day. She pointedly kept her attention on the customers, but he stopped near her window, and said in a low voice, "I see you survived the ordeal all right." She felt her face burning, and hated herself for it. He left without giving her a chance to respond, and she ignored the questioning look on Tina's face.

He fell into step with her on Thursday afternoon as she was leaving the bank and walked with her to the car. "Will you go with me to a dinner in Omaha Saturday night?" he asked. "It's a dinner meeting for eastern Nebraska bankers. It will be held on the top floor of the Woodmen of the World Building. You have a rare view of Omaha from up there."

Ginger didn't want to go to the meeting, but she did want to be with him. Still, she thought they should end their association once and for all. Somehow she had realized that, the more she saw Darren, the more she'd be hurt when he dropped her as he had everyone else. She forced herself to say, "Thank you, but I can't."

"Can't, or won't?"

"Can't!" she replied. "The class I'm taking at the university requires an extracurricular activity. Every other Saturday morning Ken and I work with a group of children."

"The dinner isn't until Saturday night," Darren persisted.

"And I have several hundred pages of reading before class on Tuesday," she continued. "I'll need to do that Saturday night. Besides, I left all of my evening clothes stored at the farm when I moved."

"I'd like for you to go," he insisted, as she got into her car. She looked him evenly in the eye after closing the door and shook her head.

On the way home, Ginger stopped at a fabric store and bought several yards of light green material. She knew that it would make a lovely evening dress—and she started working on it that night. If Darren kept insisting on her going as he had last weekend, at least she would have a suitable dress.

The next evening, when Ginger arrived home, Sally Stone emerged from her trailer. She was carrying a package. "You really are going up in the world," Sally laughingly said. "When did you start buying expensive clothes?" She handed Ginger a package from one of Lincoln's most exclusive dress shops. "This was delivered for you today."

"I haven't bought anything there," Ginger said. "They must have brought it to the wrong place. I'll check on it." She wasn't going to open the box in front of Sally, for she had a sneaking suspicion where the package had originated.

Darren's handwriting was on a card inside the box. "With my compliments!" the note crowed. "I owe you a dress to replace the new one you ruined Sunday.

I'll pick you up at three o'clock tomorrow. DB."

He has his nerve, Ginger thought as she lifted the sleek black garment out of the box. The floor-length dress was made of woven semi-sheer georgette. The strapless bodice was form-fitting, and the full skirt, while flowing floor-length in the back, came to the knees in front.

She knew she couldn't consider accepting the dress, but she locked the door against a sudden visit from Sally or Mrs. Gainer, and hurried to the bedroom to try on the garment. The fit was perfect, but she was less than pleased that Darren knew so much about women's clothes. She could see that she was stunning in such a dress; the dark fabric accentuated her pearl-white shoulders, the pinkish tint of her face, her gray eyes, and her red hair. Nevertheless, she folded the spectacular dress carefully, and replaced it in the box.

The hours that Ken and Ginger spent with the handicapped children at the gym on Saturday mornings were frustrating, but also rewarding in many ways. At the end of two hours, they were exhausted by their efforts to help the children exercise to the best of their abilities.

"How about coming out to the farm with me for the rest of the day, Ginger? Mother was making cherry pies when I left," Ken said as they left the gymnasium. "You look tired, and a change will be good for you."

"Don't tempt me, Ken. I really don't want to go home, and the thought of your mother's good cooking is hard to turn down. But I do have lots to do this afternoon. Thanks anyway." She almost wished that Ken had insisted, for she wanted to avoid the altercation with Darren that she knew would come if she stayed at home. She had to make him see that she wouldn't ac-

41

cept expensive gifts from him, so she drove back to her trailer.

Ginger had settled down to typing a school report when Mrs. Gainer knocked at the door. With an inward sigh, Ginger made the older lady welcome. As Mrs. Gainer talked, Ginger made tea and set out cookies on the table beside her neighbor.

"My dear," Mrs. Gainer said, finally coming to the reason for her visit. "I saw that dreadful Mr. Banning bringing you home the other night. I don't want to interfere in your business, but I think I should warn you about him. Especially since your mother isn't here to look after you."

Although Ginger herself had been harboring nasty thoughts about Darren all week, she still resented Mrs. Gainer's remarks. "He's president of the bank where I work, so I can hardly help meeting him occasionally. I didn't know you knew him."

Mrs. Gainer asked for another cup of tea and helped herself to two more cookies before she continued. Lowering her voice, she said, "He's a crook, Ginger!"

Ginger had expected a lecture on Darren's philandering; she *hadn't* anticipated *this* accusation! "A crook?" she asked, partly in surprise, partly in dismay. "I'd rather not hear this. After all, I do work for him, and I'd rather not gossip about my employer."

Mrs. Gainer would not be put off. "It's because you *do* work there that you should know what kind of man he is. And it isn't gossip. I know what I'm talking about. My husband and I owned stock in the Midland Bank when Mr. Banning came there about ten years ago. George and I were under obligation to Mr. Banning, who insisted on buying our stock. Finally, when George had a heart attack, and the doctor gave him only a few months to live, we signed a contract, giving

42

Mr. Banning the option to buy our stock for twenty-five dollars a share upon George's death. That was the price of the stock at that time."

I don't want to hear this, Ginger thought. She found herself torn between loyalty to Darren and sympathy for Mrs. Gainer, who obviously needed a confidante.

"But, you see, George didn't die until four months ago! When I started to settle the estate, Mr. Banning appeared with the signed contract, demanding the stock certificates! That stock represents a large part of my inheritance, and I feel sure it's worth a lot more than it was ten years ago. Mr. Banning just laughed at me when I told him that I didn't want to let the stock go at the price we had originally agreed upon."

Ginger felt sickened at the story. Surely Darren Banning wasn't the kind of man to take advantage of a widow—and, in all fairness to him, she had to admit that the Gainers *had* signed the contract.

When Ginger didn't comment, her neighbor continued, "He said 'business is business,' and that the stock should have been his years ago, as if he were sorry George hadn't died earlier! Don't you think he should pay the current price for that stock, Ginger?"

At that inopportune moment, the notorious Mr. Banning appeared at the door, and Mrs. Gainer jumped up as though she'd been stung. "I'll see you later, Ginger," she said. The widow opened the screen door and pushed by Darren without a word.

He looked after her in surprise. "What's she doing here?" he demanded. Without an invitation, he opened the door and came in.

"She lives in the trailer across the way," Ginger said.

"What was she telling you?" he demanded.

"We were just having a neighborly visit," she

evaded. "She comes over quite often, and today she came at my busiest time."

Darren looked with disfavor at her jeans and T-shirt. "Aren't you ready yet?"

"I'm ready to finish my typing, if that's what you mean." Ginger perched on the stool behind her typewriter.

"Didn't you get my note? I told you I'd be here at three o'clock."

"But I had already told you that I had work to do. If Mrs. Gainer hadn't delayed me, I might have gotten the paper done. And I also have a book to read."

He sat down on the couch. "I'll wait until you finish the paper. You can read the book tomorrow."

Ginger didn't answer, but started to type. With him glaring at her, it was difficult to keep her mind on the words. He obviously wasn't in a good humor today. She tried to ignore him, but he fidgeted around on the couch, and finally stood up and strode to the door.

He swore and said, "It's hotter than blazes in here. Why don't you turn on the air conditioner?"

Ginger rolled a new sheet of paper into the typewriter. "I don't have an air conditioner. Anyway, I'm not hot."

He sat down again, but her hands were shaking until she made error after error. In desperation, she said, "What time does that meeting start?"

"Seven o'clock," he said shortly.

Weakening, she said, "Then why is it necessary to leave so early? You can drive to Omaha in an hour."

"The social hour starts at six."

"Well, I don't want to go to the social hour," she said. "I won't know anyone there."

"But maybe *I* want to go," he answered nastily.

She was trying to be calm, but he was a most irritat-

44

I'll be gone for a few weeks, and I didn't know when I would see you again."

"Tell me about your ranch."

At last she had found a subject which he would discuss. "I call it the Golden Triangle. It's located north of Thedford in the Sand Hills. Twenty sections of the most beautiful rangeland in the world! We run several hundred head of cattle. The nearest neighbor is fifteen miles away, so, when I'm up there, I usually don't see anyone except the ranch hands."

"So that's the reason for all the golden triangles," Ginger said. "They're very eye-catching. Is there any significance to your choice?"

"It's my cattle brand for one thing." He touched the apex of the triangle on the dashboard. "This stands for the ranch. The other points represent my oil interests and the bank. They're all locked together." He talked on about the place until they reached Omaha.

Unfortunately, as far as Ginger was concerned, they weren't late enough to miss the social hour. Darren was most attentive, and introduced her to his friends, but Ginger was uncomfortable. Many of his friends looked surprised to see her, and one man peered at her and said, "Why, this is a new one, Banning! What happened to Maureen?"

Darren gave him a murderous look, and led Ginger away to find a seat in the dining area. He was careful to find a place where she could look out over the lighted city. Darren was obviously enraged by the man's remarks, and she wondered if he thought she was unaware that Maureen normally accompanied him.

"You needn't mind what your friend said. I know that Maureen is your usual companion at these functions. Couldn't she come tonight?"

"I didn't ask her," he said shortly.

47

"She won't like the fact that you brought me."

Ginger heard his muttered oath as he turned away a moment. "Maureen, or no other woman for that matter, has any hold on me. Forget it!"

Fortunately, at that time, the food service began, and the subject was dropped, but not forgotten—at least, not on Ginger's part. The food and the nighttime view of Omaha were magnificent. She listened eagerly to the speaker, for she wanted to learn about the things that interested Darren.

Darren chatted about the meeting during their drive back to Lincoln, but Ginger said little. *How intelligent the man is*! she thought. Although she wasn't sure of the tactics he'd used to gain influence in the financial world, she did admire his ability. What a pity that he didn't use his talents to benefit others rather than just Darren Banning.

The hour was past midnight when they arrived in Lincoln. Darren walked with her to the door of the trailer and waited until she'd unlocked it. She didn't turn on the lamp inside the door because the hall light was on.

"Thank you for a nice evening," Ginger said.

"May I come in for a while?"

"Please, no," Ginger answered. "It's late, and I am tired."

But, he pushed open the door, followed her into the dimly lighted room, and closed the door behind them. "Not even for a goodnight kiss?" he asked.

Ginger cringed at his words, not sure how to reply.

Darren held out his arms to her, and, when she stood rooted to the floor, he drew her somewhat roughly into his embrace.

Ginger stood unyielding, hating herself for her lack

of response, and thinking, *Don't be a child. He only wants to kiss you. After all, you owe him that much for his attention to you.*

But she was afraid. She hoped the fear didn't show in her eyes when she hesitantly raised her face toward him. Darren's lips were warm and tender as they moved over her frigid mouth. He drew back and looked wonderingly at her for a moment. He lowered his head again, and this time his kiss became passionate and demanding, as he tried to draw a response from her. He lifted her from the floor and molded her body tightly against his.

Cold chills coursed through Ginger Wilson's veins and her throat constricted as the past came back to haunt her. No longer was she in her own home with a man she admired. No longer was she in the arms of Darren Banning, the most handsome man she knew. The years rolled back as she relived that horrible moment when another man had awakened her with his sweating, amorous, revolting caresses.

She sensed the scream starting in the recesses of her mind, and, when Darren raised his mouth momentarily, her revulsion erupted into a maddening, uncontrollable screech. Darren clapped his hand over her mouth, and shook her.

"Stop it, you little idiot! What's the matter with you? I was only kissing you."

Ginger was sobbing now, and she broke away from his grasp, and ran in terror to the bedroom, calling as she went, "Leave me alone! Go home! Go home!" She collapsed on the bed, trembling, her body contorted by deep sobs.

Darren didn't go home. He followed her down the hallway, but he made no move to touch her. His voice was kind as he spoke from the doorway. "Ginger, I

49

meant no harm to you. Why are you acting this way?"

Ginger's cries came louder and louder. Now she was weeping partly because she'd made such a fool of herself, but mostly because she had lost all self-control.

The telephone by her bedside rang. After it rang several times, and she made no move to answer, Darren picked up the receiver.

Ginger heard Sally's voice on the line. "Is Ginger there?"

"Yes," Darren answered shortly.

"May I speak to her, please?"

Ginger shook her head. Apparently Darren couldn't see in the dim light, for he handed her the receiver. Ginger sat up and tried to control her trembling lips as she answered.

She was still sobbing, and Sally's voice was full of concern. "Are you all right? I thought I heard you scream."

"I'm fine. Nothing is wrong."

"Who's there with you?"

"Mr. Banning is here. We just got back from Omaha, and he's getting ready to leave. I'll see you in the morning." She hung up the receiver and prostrated herself on the bed again.

"You surely have a lot of privacy!" Darren muttered. He sat beside her on the bed and patted her trembling back. His hands were comforting, but the shaking continued. He spoke soothingly. "Ginger, I meant no harm. I wanted to kiss you because I'm so fond of you."

His words were pleasant to Ginger's ears. "Please go home," she managed to say. "I'll be all right." She was beginning to be sick at her stomach, which always happened when she cried so hard. Already embarrassed enough, Ginger had to get rid of him before she got sick.

"I wouldn't think of leaving you in such a shape. When you settle down, I'll leave, but not before."

Hot, acid liquid began to swell in her throat, and she broke out into a cold sweat. Ginger pushed his hands aside, scrambled off the bed, and ran retching into the bathroom. She managed to reach the toilet before she vomited. Even at that, the vomit splashed onto the floor and all over the front of her new dress. Another dress ruined!

She sat weakly on a stool by the shower after her stomach was emptied. The stench in the room was terrible when Darren appeared at the door and fumbled for the light switch. Ginger couldn't look up. Would the man leave her no pride at all? She would never be able to look him in the face again!

Darren took a cloth from the rack, wet it under the faucet, and knelt by her side. "Be careful of your clothes," she whispered, but he appeared unaware of the condition of the room. He smoothed back her hair, and wiped her face with the cool cloth, murmuring softly to her as if she were a child.

"And you've made a mess of your pretty dress, too," Darren said. "Want to get back in bed now?" When she nodded, he guided her gently to the bedroom. He left the room when she was lying down again, and Ginger hoped he was going home. However, she heard him open the refrigerator. Ice clinked into a glass, and soon he returned. Darren sat on the bed, lifted her, and held his arm around her for support. "Here, drink this 7-Up to settle your stomach."

She sipped the cool drink gratefully, and it lessened the foul taste in her mouth. When she indicated that she'd had enough, Darren let her lie back and placed the glass on the nightstand. "Let's leave it here. You may want some more later. Feeling better?" he inquired.

The vomiting seemed to have calmed her somewhat, and her trembling was lessening. He went into the bathroom and returned with her nightgown, which had been hanging behind the door.

"Why don't you get out of your clothes, and get ready for bed? When you're asleep, I'll leave."

Is he going to stand there and watch me undress? she wondered. Her hands fumbled, trying to undo the buttons at the back, but Darren brushed her hands aside, unfastened the dress, and pulled it over her head, while she stood humiliated and trembling at his side. When his hands moved to her slip, she whispered, "Oh, please, don't. I'll manage."

Without argument, he took her dress and went into the bathroom. While she hurried as fast as she could to get into her gown, she heard him running water in the lavatory. She was covered in bed when he came back with the dress over his arm. Darren opened the closet door, found a hanger, and placed the green dress on it. "I washed the stain out of your dress, and I think it will be all right. I'll hang it in the bathroom to dry. If you keep going out with me," he muttered, "you won't have any clothes left!"

While she lay in silence, he returned to the bathroom, and again she heard running water. From the sounds, she guessed that he was cleaning the soiled floor! Ginger couldn't believe this was happening.

What kind of man was he anyway? She felt as though she were on a game show, trying to choose the real Mr. Banning. He had so many faces: the angry employer, the hard-fisted banker and businessman, the attentive companion, the successful rancher, and now the compassionate friend. "Will the real Mr. Banning please stand up?" Of all his characters, which *was* the real Mr. Banning? Probably somewhere in between his outward appearances, she surmised. She wondered if he'd ever reveal his true nature to her.

Coming back into the bedroom, Darren sat down on the bed and ran a hand over her arm. She flinched until she realized that his touch was tender and impersonal, merely trying to see if she were still shaking. He felt her forehead and smoothed the hair back from her face. "Are you still nauseated?" he inquired.

"No," Ginger whispered weakly.

"I'm going to turn out the light and go to the other part of the house. You try to sleep, and, when I'm sure you're all right, I'll go home. OK?"

She nodded and rubbed her face against his hand. "I'm sorry I've been so much trouble."

He patted her affectionately on the shoulder, and turned off the light. The illuminated face of her clock showed two-thirty. Ginger was far from going to sleep, but she didn't want him to know that. She lay as still as possible.

Almost an hour later, Darren walked softly to her door and listened. Not by a twitch did she indicate that she was still awake, so he went back into the living room and left the house. Soon she heard the big car easing away from the trailer court.

She smiled to herself, knowing that, if her neighbors had noted his late departure, her reputation would be in shreds. Lying awake for a long time and thinking of him, Ginger compared Mrs. Gainer's assessment of Darren to his kindness toward her tonight amid a situation that he couldn't possibly have understood.

"The dreadful Mr. Banning indeed!" she murmured.

Chapter Four

When morning came, Ginger got up as usual and drove to church, in spite of the fact that she hadn't had an hour's sleep all night. Sally eyed her unusual pallor and sunken eyes inquisitively, but asked no questions. Ginger might as well have stayed at home for all the good the sermon did her. She simply couldn't concentrate on the sermon. Her mind was on Darren, wondering if she'd ever see him again. If he *did* come back, how could she explain her actions of the night before?

He was waiting in his car when she got home from church. Perhaps not knowing what his reception would be, he didn't get out of the car when she pulled up. She walked over to him, and, at first, neither of them said anything. From the weariness around his eyes, she surmised that he hadn't slept any more than she had.

Ginger placed her hand on the open car window, and he covered it with his. "I'm going to the ranch early in the morning, but I couldn't leave with everything so unsettled between us. I know I've ruined your weekend, but do you have a few hours for me?

Do you have to study?" His voice was pleading—a new manner for him.

"I'm too tired to study. I ... ? with you."

"Do you want to change into something comfortable? Since it's so warm, I stopped at a restaurant and had a picnic lunch packed."

"I'll only be a few minutes. Maybe I can take a book along and study a little anyway."

Since Darren was dressed in jeans, Ginger slipped into a teal mini-culotte skirt and a white top with puffed sleeves and banded cuffs and bottom. She pulled on tennis shoes and also took a three-cornered scarf to wear if the wind became too strong.

"That didn't take long," he observed as she came hurrying back. Ginger waved to Mrs. Gainer, who was peering out the window as usual, and called to the Stones, who were just driving into their yard. "We're going on a picnic. I'll be back before church time."

Before they got to the highway, Darren said, "Do you know anyplace we can go to get away from people for a while? I've had about enough of this town!"

"Have you been to the state park near Louisville?"

"No."

"Our church went down there for an outing a few weeks ago," Ginger said. "There are hiking trails and many tables for picnicking."

"That sounds like the ideal place." After they'd driven several miles, Darren reached out his arm to her, and said, "You seem so far away." She hesitated only a moment before she slid across the car seat and into the circle of his arm. As he tightened his grip, Ginger had the feeling that she'd arrived at home for the first time. With a sigh, she leaned against him and became oblivious to her surroundings until Darren shook her lightly.

"Ginger, wake up, and tell me if we take this next road to the park. We're almost to Louisville." With her head resting on his shoulder, she had slept for almost an hour.

Ginger straightened up and apologized. "I didn't mean to go to sleep!"

He grinned at her. "No matter, but you've about paralyzed my arm. Lean up a bit." It was surprising that she trusted herself so easily to him.

In spite of the lovely weather, there were only a few other cars in the parking lot, and the trails weren't crowded. Darren carried their box lunch, and Ginger led the way up a trail through oak forests. They caught only an occasional glimpse of the Platte River, until they came to an open bluff, affording a panoramic view of the river valley. No one else was in sight, and they sat on the open hillside to eat their lunch. Darren had ordered a complete feast—fried chicken, rolls, cole slaw, baked beans, iced tea, and some mouth-watering lemon pastries for dessert. They ate undistrubed except for a feisty chickadee clamoring above their heads.

When the food was gone, Darren stretched out on the ground and went to sleep. Ginger picked up the book she'd brought along and tried to read. She finally gave it up as useless, thinking that, if she continued to see Darren, she would flunk out of school!

Leaning back against a tree, she allowed herself the pleasure of watching him—his rugged handsomeness made her breathe faster. His blue knit shirt was open at the neck, and the even rise and fall of his chest fascinated her. He looked a bit strange in the faded denims and jogging shoes, as he usually was dressed in tailored garments; but, to her, no one else had ever graced denims in such a wonderful way. Ginger pon-

He groaned. "I might have known."

Ginger was roused by the ringing of the phone. "Happy twenty-fourth birthday," her mother's voice sounded in her ears.

Ginger awakened immediately. "Mother! Are you calling from Saudi Arabia?"

"Yes, and I wasn't sure of the time difference. What time is it over there?"

Ginger looked at the clock. "Four o'clock in the morning." She longed to tell her mother about the frustrating situation with Darren, but she realized that she couldn't explain it all over the phone.

"Are you having any vacation time this year?" her mother asked.

"I think I'll have a week or so in August, but I'm not sure."

"John and I would love to have you come here for a visit. We'll help pay your fare. I don't think we'll be home for another two years."

"Thanks, Mother, but I'm sure I can't come this year. I'm getting along all right."

The phone call was all too short, but it did help Ginger to face her first birthday since her grandmother's death. And bless Sally, who had asked her over for the evening meal! She wouldn't have to eat alone anyway.

Ginger knew that the bank would seem empty without Darren, but, in a way, she was relieved that he was going away. When she drove into the bank's parking lot, however, his car was in its usual place. Entering the bank, she encountered him in the foyer. His face looked as if it had been etched in granite, and the expression in his eyes was deadly. She knew better than to ask any questions, but he volunteered, "I didn't get to leave after all. These idiots around here are about to drive me to the poorhouse." He brushed on by her, and ran down the steps.

Tina Alleman was at her window when Ginger arrived, and she lifted her eyebrows in a suggestive gesture. "Walk easy today," she said. "The Big Boss is on the warpath."

While Ginger prepared her cash drawer and checked her supplies for the day's work, she wondered what had happened to put Darren in such a vile mood. His temper had affected the whole staff, and everyone worked in silence.

Darren came striding back into the bank shortly before opening time and went to the note department. The escalator was too slow for him, so he bounded up the steps. Occasionally his angry voice wafted from one of the offices.

When he left the note department, his austere frame appeared on the mezzanine, and he could be heard delivering a booming ultimatum. "If we don't get that account back, I'm warning you, I'll dispose of this whole outfit by the end of the week!"

During their lunch break, while Ginger and Tina were in the lounge alone, Ginger whispered, "What *is* going on?"

"I don't have all the facts, but it seems one of the loan officers let a tremendous deal get away from the bank, costing us several hundred thousand dollars, and Banning only learned about it last night. He's already fired the loan officer, and God help us *all* if he doesn't get that account back!"

And God help me, Ginger prayed to herself. *Why did I ever get mixed up with such a paradox of a man?*

She dreaded an encounter with him during the day, but, at noon, he left alone. By closing time he hadn't returned. She left the building with a sense of relief

60

when the day's work was over. She supposed that Darren finally had gone to his ranch, and she had escaped angering him.

The minute that Ginger stepped inside her home, she realized that something was wrong. It took another moment for her to realize what it was. The trailer was much *cooler* than outside—and she discovered an *air conditioner* installed in the utility room!

Going to the phone, she called Sally. "Do you know who has been in my home today?" she asked.

"The air conditioning men came and asked me to let them in. They said they had a unit to install for you. Is anything wrong?"

"Sally, I didn't order that air conditioner."

Her friend gasped. "Why, Ginger, I had no idea. What's going on?"

Ginger knew immediately who had ordered the air conditioner, and she didn't like it. "Well, never mind, Sally, but please don't accept anything else from anyone for me, or let anyone in my home again unless I tell you."

"I'm really sorry, Ginger. Dinner will be ready about six o'clock. Is that all right with you?"

"Fine," she replied. "See you soon."

Ginger angrily switched off the air conditioning unit. What was the man trying to do, anyway? He must have known that she wouldn't want him to buy her such a gift.

She tried to forget Darren and the problems he had caused her while she ate with her friends. Sally and Roger had invited Ken, and, after the tension at the bank all day, Ginger was able to relax in the fellowship with the friends she admired so much.

Sally had a buffet meal of ham, baked beans, sweet

potatoes, and a relish tray. They served themselves from the kitchen counter and ate at both TV tables and the small kitchen table. From his high chair, Patrick got more than his share of food, as each person placed tidbits on his plate.

They were just ready for dessert when Sally glanced out the window, and said to Ginger, "Oh, oh! You have company."

Ginger's face flushed as she spied the white Cadillac in front of her trailer. Darren was standing on the porch ringing her doorbell.

"I thought he was gone," she said in dismay.

She went out on the steps and called, "I'm over here, Mr. Banning."

As he walked across the small area separating the two trailers, the look on his face wasn't encouraging.

"I'm having dinner with the Stones."

"I'm surprised that you can leave your studies to visit anyone." His tone implied that her need to study was just an excuse used on him.

Ginger answered lightly, "I accepted Sally's invitation last week. That's why I needed to study over the weekend."

Sally appeared at the door. "Come on in, Mr. Banning. We're celebrating Ginger's birthday. There's plenty of food left for you."

Darren gave Ginger a reproachful look. "No, thank you, I've already eaten."

But it wasn't easy to shrug off Sally's friendliness. "At least, come in for birthday cake and ice cream," she persisted. "We're just ready for it."

He obviously had no desire to do so, but he entered the room, and, if he was bored, at least he behaved himself. He visited pleasantly with Roger, who had once lived in the Sand Hills area where Darren's ranch was located. He complimented Sally on the cake, but, as soon as it was decently possible, he stood to leave.

"Kiss, good-bye," Patrick, sitting in the high chair, held up his arms and cried to Darren, but the man turned abruptly and ignored the child. *That would be expecting just a bit too much*, Ginger supposed.

She walked to the door with him and said good-bye briefly.

Oh, God, Ginger prayed silently as she watched him drive away, *give me the wisdom to point him in the right direction. He never leaves, but that I wonder if he'll ever return*. She went back inside, and, with an effort, remained cheerful the rest of the evening. But Sally was not fooled. As Ginger left for home, her friend whispered, "I'm sorry we ruined your evening with him."

Ginger hugged her and said, "You've said it the wrong way. *He* almost ruined my evening with *you*. Thanks for everything, Sally."

The big Cadillac wasn't in its usual place the next morning, and Ginger assumed that Darren was at last on his way out of town. Tina relayed the latest news while they arranged their currency for the day.

"We're back in business, I guess. The Big Boss himself regained that real estate account. I don't know how many people he knifed in the back, or how much blackmail he used, but at least the note department employees are safe."

"What about the man he fired yesterday?"

"I got my information from one of the secretaries upstairs," Tina replied, "and she said Banning absolutely refused to have him on the premises again. With him, you don't get a second chance!"

Ginger pondered that grim statement most of the

morning. Their friendship, or *whatever* existed between them, hung by a slim thread. One day at a time was about all she could expect with him.

Acting upon the assumption that Darren was gone, the downstairs employees were more lighthearted than they had been yesterday. Thus, Ginger gasped in surprise when she looked up to see Darren standing in front of her window.

"When is your lunch period, Miss Wilson?"

Ginger glanced at the clock. "In a half-hour."

"Please come to my office for a few minutes then." He turned and strode rapidly across the lobby and into his office. Ginger watched his departure, noting that he didn't even look at Maureen as he passed her desk.

Tina whistled under her breath. "What have you done now?" she muttered. "It seems you're rating more than your share of attention from the Big Boss."

The next thirty minutes seemed to stretch interminably, but, when the time came to go to Darren's office, Ginger wished that she could delay even longer. Maureen Rowley gave Ginger a look of pure malice as she approached the office. Ginger wanted to say, "It isn't my fault. Don't blame me." But she said nothing as she knocked and entered the plush office.

Darren sat behind the desk, his hands clasped before him. He stared at her pensively, that sadness back in his dark eyes again, as Ginger sat before him. His look was making her uncomfortable, and she dropped her gaze and clenched her hands in her lap.

When he continued to stare, she said in the lightest possible tone, "I only have a short lunch period. Did you want to talk with me, or just look at me?"

"Why didn't you tell me yesterday was your birthday?" he demanded gruffly.

"I didn't tell anyone. Sally found out when I put my

birthday offering in our church collection last week."

He opened a desk drawer and took out a small box, with the name of Lincoln's most expensive jeweler on the outside. He handed it to her, but she couldn't seem to unclench her hands to take the box.

With a slight smile, he said, "A belated Happy Birthday."

When she still hesitated, he said harshly, "Take it!"

With fumbling fingers, she opened the box, and gasped at its contents—a white gold chain woven around twelve miniature emeralds! In the middle of the emeralds there hung a diamond pendant which was bigger than the end of her little finger!

She looked at him, chagrin mirrored on her face.

"What's the matter? Don't you like it?"

"Certainly I like it. Who wouldn't? It's beautiful, but I don't have any use for a necklace like this. It's too valuable to leave around the house."

"Don't leave it around the house. Wear it!"

"Where would I wear it?" Ginger responded. "Anyplace I go—to church, to school, to work—this jewelry would be out of place."

He came around the desk to her, removed the simple chain she wore, took the necklace from its box, and placed it around her neck. Pulling her upward, he turned her to face a mirror behind the door. The necklace stood out vividly against her black cotton blouse. Ginger knew that she couldn't accept his gift. "You shouldn't have bought me such an expensive gift."

"What did Ken give you?" he demanded, causing her to wonder if he were jealous of Ken.

"A bottle of Avon perfume, but—"

"And I'll bet that strained his finances more than this necklace did mine." He turned her to face him, held her at arm's length, and admired the necklace.

"Wear it, Ginger. It's perfect with your coloring. I want to give you gifts!"

She lifted troubled eyes to his. "Please don't make me wear it out there." She motioned toward the bank's lobby.

"Make you!" He swore a vicious oath, and Ginger flinched at hearing God's name uttered so carelessly. "Most women would give their right arm for a piece of jewelry like that. I paid a thousand dollars for that necklace."

"A thousand-dollar necklace on a ten-dollar blouse," she said with a little laugh. "Even you must see how ridiculous it is. I can't accept it. Such jewelry is wasted on me."

Without a word, he spun her around roughly, removed the necklace, and threw it into a drawer. He sat down at the desk, and started figuring on some papers before him. Ginger assumed that the interview was terminated from his point of view, but she stood, her hands on his desk, before him. "I just can't understand you," she said.

He was definitely angry. His eyes were stormy and his lips were drawn in such a firm line under the mustache that white tension furrows stood out in his dark face. "What is that supposed to mean?" he demanded.

"You think nothing of spending a thousand dollars for a piece of jewelry that I don't want or need. Yet you fire a man who has a family to support simply because he made a mistake in judgment, when you thought it would cost this corporation a little money."

"A little money! Do you call $500,000 a little money?" he said with a nasty laugh. "Although what I do is none of your business, let me tell you that I don't mix pleasure and business. If I want to spend money for something that gives me pleasure, I'll do it, but I'm

man in your position not care about his reputation?"

"We're getting away from the subject. Are you going with me to New Orleans or not?"

"No."

"What if I say you're going *or else*?" he demanded, and Ginger almost quailed before the venom in his eyes.

Tears were stinging her eyelids, she was trembling inside, and the palms of her hands were wet. Yet Ginger's throat was so dry that she spoke with difficulty. "I suppose you're threatening to fire me. But if my continued employment at Midland Bank depends on becoming your lover, I might as well leave now, for that will never happen! I've saved enough money to get along until I find another job."

"I have enough influence in this city that I can keep you from getting work anywhere!" he asserted.

"I don't believe that. God takes care of me, and I don't believe you're as powerful as God, even though you seem to think you are."

"Don't start preaching your religious dogma to me. Power comes from money, Miss Wilson. I have enough money to buy anything I want."

"Your money doesn't impress me. As far as I'm concerned, you're the poorest man I know." Ginger wondered how much more of this tension she could stand.

"For one last time," he thundered, "are you going with me?"

"NO!"

"Then get out of here, Miss Prude!"

"Not until I'm finished." Her voice was shaking now, and she pressed her lips to still their trembling. "I wouldn't have the kind of relationship you suggest with any man, and especially one I can't respect."

"And why don't I merit your respect?" he asked sardonically.

"Because you're only interested in what benefits Darren Banning. No matter whom you trample underfoot, you're going to get what you want. If you want to impress me, pay Mrs. ___ainer what her bank stock is worth, instead of trying to cheat her out of her inheritance."

"So she did tell you," he said.

"And as for all your money, I can think of many things it can't buy—peace of mind, happiness, and the respect of other people to name only a few. And it can't buy *me*, so please leave me alone!"

Ginger resumed her work with an effort, but her hands shook as she opened her window. She was, on the one hand, amazed at her boldness and, on the other, afraid her harsh words had ended something that had become vital and precious to her life.

She drove slowly to work the next morning, wishing she had the backbone to leave the Midland Bank. Surely she could find another job somewhere. She stopped at a red light near Lincoln's city limits, and, while she waited for the light to turn, she glanced at the telephone booth beside the highway. *Why not just telephone and say I'm quitting?* But that seemed a coward's way out, and when the light turned green, she drove on.

Suddenly she observed a car coming rapidly toward her from a road that crossed the intersection at an angle. Before she knew what was happening, the large car crashed into the left front of her Volkswagen. The sound of breaking glass and crushing metal stunned her, and for a moment she wasn't able to move. When she did step from her car, the driver of the other vehicle rushed toward her. "Now look what you've done," he shouted. "Pulled right out in front of me."

"But I had the right-of-way," Ginger protested. "The light was green."

"So *you* say. I had the green light."

No one else had witnessed the accident, and Ginger realized that it would be her word against his. She cringed when she saw the damage to her new automobile. The bumper was loose, and the right headlight was turned sideways.

A truck driver called as he passed slowly, "Having trouble, buddy? I'll notify the cops on my CB."

The word "cop" startled Ginger more than ever. She hadn't been in an accident before, and she couldn't remember the steps she needed to take. The bigger car had sustained very little damage, but the driver exclaimed loudly over the scratches on his car and asserted his innocence to anyone who stopped. Ginger was almost in tears, but she was determined not to cry. She suffered his accusations in silence, thinking that she'd save her argument for the police. Glancing at her watch, she could see she would be late for work, and she walked toward the phone booth.

"You come back here," the man shouted. "Don't you leave the scene of an accident."

Ginger ignored him. She was trying to be calm, but her hands shook until she could hardly dial the number. Her voice sounded unnatural and strained when she finally reached Tina.

"I'm going to be late for work, Tina. I've had an accident."

"Where?" Tina demanded.

"Just west of town near the intersection of Routes 2 and 6. I'm waiting for the police to come now."

"What happened? Are you hurt? Do you need any help?" Tina questioned in rapid succession.

"I can't talk anymore," Ginger responded. "I hear the police siren, so I'd better get back to my car. I'll be there as soon as I can." But Ginger took time for a short prayer for strength and guidance before she left the phone booth.

As the officer stepped from the patrol car, the man who'd hit Ginger's car immediately nailed him. "I had the green light, and this woman drove right in front of me."

By that time several curious spectators had gathered, and they all seemed to be looking at Ginger with accusing eyes. The policeman asked to see her license and the car registration. He seemed to believe everything the man told him. Ginger really became alarmed when the officer mentioned giving her a citation, but she didn't realize how alone she felt until she saw a white Cadillac speeding down the road. It came to a sudden halt behind the police crusier, and when Darren stepped out of the car, she ran toward him, her tears beginning to flow. He opened his arms, and she leaned against him sobbing. His arms tightened protectively, and said, "Are you hurt, Ginger?"

"No, but I'm scared!" she sobbed.

"Well, stop being scared. I'm here now. What happened?"

"I drove through the intersection when the light turned green, and that other car banged into me. Now the driver's telling everyone that I ran a red light, and the policeman is writing *me* a citation."

He swore in his habitual manner. "We'll see about that. Come on."

His arm still around her, he led her toward the others. If Ginger had ever questioned the tremendous power Darren wielded in that city, she would never doubt it again. While he silently surveyed the scene dered how quickly she had become sensitive to his presence. He was certainly not a man of whom she approved, but he was one who was beginning to dominate her life.

She was still watching him when he opened his eyes and spied her. His gaze held unfathomable meaning, and she wished that she knew what he was thinking.

She was the first to look away. "I think I owe you an explanation about last night," Ginger began.

He smiled wanly, as he rolled over on his side and pillowed his head on his arms. "Well, my male ego has been irreparably damaged, because my advances have never created such a fracas before. I must be losing my charm."

"No, you still have *too much* of that." She flashed him a slight smile, but still she hesitated. "Remembering a terrible experience of the past caused my hysteria last night, and it's hard for me to talk about it."

"Don't, if you'd rather not. You don't have to tell me anything," he assured her.

"But I think it's time I talked about it," Ginger said. With an effort, she began, "My first stepfather tried to…assault me when I was twelve years old. I awakened one night to find him in bed with me, and his caresses were so repulsive." She shuddered. "No one had kissed me like that since that time. Last night, it all came back to me."

"That isn't very flattering."

"I know I'm telling this badly," she apologized. "You don't remind me of him at all; it isn't that. Anyway, Mother heard me screaming and came in before he could…" Ginger covered her face with her hands, finding it difficult to continue. She couldn't look at Darren. "We left that night for my grandmother's. My mother divorced him, and I never saw him again, but

57

Mother and Grandmother always acted as if it hadn't happened. Apparently they thought I'd forget it if they didn't talk about it! Sometimes I believe it would have been better if they'd talked to me about the situation. Today is the first time I've mentioned the incident to anyone."

"I'm sorry I caused you to remember it at all," Darren offered, gazing at her.

Ginger sat silently while the breeze from the Platte valley tossed her hair. "No, it's time I faced my frustrations over it. Frankly, I've been afraid to date anyone."

He moved nearer to Ginger and took her hand. "Maybe that's just as well. Otherwise, you'd have had so many admirers, you wouldn't have given me a second look."

"I doubt it," Ginger laughed and decided that he could take her meaning as he liked.

He lifted her hand and kissed it lightly. "I'd like to wring the scoundrel's neck, but I'll try to make it up to you." He jumped to his feet. "Let's hike for awhile before we go home."

He was a pleasant companion for the rest of the day, and no more was said about the night before. They returned to Lincoln in late afternoon. Darren didn't get out of the car, nor did he try to kiss her good-bye. But the look in his eyes set her blood racing, when he said, "With all the peeping toms you have around here, I can't do much but say good-bye. I'm going to miss you, Ginger."

"How long will you be gone?"

"Two or three weeks, I suppose. I have to go to Texas on business after I leave the ranch. By then your final exams should be over. Maybe you'll have some time for me the rest of the summer."

"But I'm taking a Saturday class this summer."

before him, Ginger observed an immediate difference in the attitude of the crowd. Obviously the policeman and the man who'd struck her car knew who Darren was.

"What's going on here?" Darren demanded.

The policeman cleared his throat twice before he answered. "Well, Mr. Banning, there's been a little accident."

"I can see *that*, but I want to know why you're giving Miss Wilson a citation."

"I didn't know she was a friend of yours, Mr. Banning."

Darren's voice was icy. "What difference does that make? A fool could see what happened here."

The officer tried to placate him. "This gentleman is a prominent farmer in the county, and I had no reason to doubt his word."

Darren's arm tightened around Ginger. "And I know this lady," he said bluntly, "and if she said that light was green when she drove through it, the light was green!"

Ginger glanced at the "prominent farmer," who hadn't said a word since Darren came. *Probably owes Midland a lot of money*, she surmised.

The policeman spoke again. "May we can just forget it, since there weren't any witnesses, or any injuries."

Darren inspected Ginger's Volkswagen thoroughly. "I don't know whether we're going to forget it or not. He may have to pay for the damage to her car. Do you have collision insurance, Ginger?"

She handed him the insurance card from her purse, and he looked it over. "This should be good enough to cover the damage, but," and he turned to the officer again, "I want this accident written up accurately, and a copy of it sent to me, so I can see what you've reported. If you make any accusations against her, you're going to answer to me."

He got in the Volkswagen and backed it away from the other vehicle. "It seems to drive all right, but you can't travel at night until you get that headlight fixed. You follow me, and we'll see about having the car repaired. I know a private garage where they work on VW's." He looked at her carefully. "Are you sure you feel like going to work? I can take you home, if you'd rather."

"No, I'm all right. I wouldn't have gotten upset if he hadn't been so nasty."

Following him into the city, Ginger flushed when she remembered how she'd run into his arms. After the quarrels they'd had recently, what had he thought? She had certainly made a spectacle of herself, but why had he come to help her?

When they arrived at the garage, Darren took charge of the negotiations as if he had every right to handle her affairs. The manager of the shop made a quick estimate of the damage and said he could have the car repaired in three days.

"That's all right, if you loan her a car to drive while you work on this one."

"Oh, we never do that, Mr. Banning. We aren't in the car rental business, you know."

"Nonsense!" Darren retorted. "You have a used car business on the other side of town, don't you? It won't hurt you to let her have one of those cars for a few days. I happen to know where you get the money to keep that place financed."

So this is how he coerces people into doing what he wants, Ginger thought, *and why he expects me to submit the same way*. She didn't like his highhanded methods on her behalf, but she felt helpless to protest.

The manager laughed nervously. "If you put it that way, Mr. Banning, I don't have much choice."

"Good," Darren said, as he ushered Ginger toward the Cadillac. "Bring a car like the one she has to Midland Bank by three o'clock this afternoon."

Ginger sat silently beside him as he steered the Cadillac through Lincoln's traffic. She wanted to voice her appreciation, but she seemed tongue-tied. When he parked at the bank, she turned toward him with a slight smile. "Thank you."

All morning he hadn't once smiled, and Ginger decided he was still mad at her, for he said gruffly, "Don't mention it."

He made no move to get out of the car, so Ginger remained seated also. Finally Darren said in a patronizing tone, "Miss Wilson, considering our conversation yesterday, and your disparaging comparison of *my* power to that of your God, I hope this little experience has taught you a thing or two. God wasn't much help to you this morning, and you can see now why money and power are beneficial, can't you?"

She shook her head, and said softly, "No."

"No!" he exploded. "Can you deny that if it hadn't been for me, you'd be cooling your heels at the police station right now?"

"You're right about that, of course. You'll never know how happy I was to see you, and I appreciate it very much."

"Well then?" he said quizzically.

"But I'm not giving you all the credit for it. You see, I *prayed* for God to send some help, and He sent *you*."

He stared at her, stark amazement mirrored upon his face. Finally he muttered, "That beats anything I've ever heard! You're hopeless."

Darren slammed the door angrily when he got out,

but after he had circled the car and opened her door, he hugged her slightly when she stood beside him.

"Anyway, Miss Prude, I'm glad you weren't hurt," he said softly. But his voice became gruff and uncompromising as he followed her into the bank. "Will you see if you can stay out of trouble for a few days? I'm too busy to come running every time you need help."

"Yes, sir," she replied meekly. She wasn't intimidated by his words and tone. She remembered how he'd come speeding to her aid, and she knew he was still interested in her despite her failure to succumb to his every desire.

Tina winked at her when she entered the teller's area, and whispered, "He's really got a bad case on you. He was talking to one of our richest depositors when I reported your accident, and he turned his back on the man, who was in the middle of a sentence, and ran out the door like he'd been shot out of a gun. Yes, he really has it bad."

Darren ignored her the rest of the week, but Ginger was still lighthearted. *He'll come back to me on my terms*, she kept telling herself. But when Friday came, and he left for New Orleans taking Maureen with him, Ginger was plunged into despair.

She tried to conceal her distress, but she realized that she hadn't been successful when Tina passed by and squeezed her around the shoulders. She whispered for Ginger's ears alone, "They always take separate rooms, you know, so maybe it isn't as bad as it looks."

Chapter Five

Darren had been back at work several days before he gave any sign that he knew Ginger existed. She tried to pretend it didn't matter, but even her sleep was troubled. In her dreams, he seemed to beckon to her, but, although she struggled to reach him, he was always beyond her grasp. Ginger hadn't lasted as long as most of his women. In less than a month he'd had enough of her.

One day, however, when she'd forgotten him for the moment, she answered the phone at her teller's station and heard his crisp voice. "Miss Wilson, will you come to my office, please?" Darren asked. His voice was cold and formal, making it more of a command than a request.

Maureen eyed her coldly as she entered his office, but, for once, her attitude didn't bother Ginger. Darren looked up at her approach, and Ginger studied every feature of the face that had been haunting her dreams. Why did he have to be so desirable, she thought, and why did her heart do such crazy things when she was around him? She could resist his charm much easier if only her heart would behave.

"Miss Wilson, do you suppose it would strain your

moral principles too much to go with me to a rodeo at North Platte tomorrow?"

A smile of joy slowly emerged on her face.

"It's a family-type entertainment, and there will be hundreds of people around, so being with me shouldn't damage your reputation too much," he added caustically.

She ignored his sarcasm, for she would forgive him anything today. Ginger hesitated. She and Ken didn't have to work at the gym, but she did have to study. *Maybe if I work extra late tonight and study Sunday afternoon, I can go with him.*

Darren obviously took her hesitation as an indication that she wouldn't go, for he cursed and said angrily, "Well, blast it, do you want to go, or don't you?"

Ginger smiled, and said softly, "Thank you very much, Mr. Banning. I'd love to go. I've never been to a rodeo."

He flushed a little and replied, "Well, why didn't you say so, then?"

Ginger's smile grew broader, and he scowled at her. "What's so funny?"

"You," Ginger laughingly said. "I'm plainly not the type of girl you like, and I have no intention of changing. I wonder why you bother with me."

His eyes were as hard as steel. "Don't think I haven't been asking myself the same question! I don't remember when I've ever encountered a more obstinate, irritating woman." He glared at her. "Now, stop that grinning and get out of here. I'm busy." He dropped his head and began to sort some papers on his desk. "I'll come for you at nine o'clock."

Ginger turned to leave. She paused with her hand on the doorknob and announced, "I'll be ready this time, but don't ask me to go anyplace with you again

78

unless you stop swearing in my presence. I don't like it."

His head came up swiftly as though she'd struck him, and his eyes shot angry darts at her. Before he could retort, she opened the door and made a quick exit.

Ginger felt carefree and frothy the rest of the afternoon. She didn't realize how evident it was until their work was finished, and Tina walked with her to the parking lot. "Don't let him hurt you, Ginger."

Startled, Ginger asked, "What do you mean?"

"I wasn't aware of the great effect he had on you until today," Tina said. "You've been rather glum all week, but, after you went to the Big Boss's office, you came out a different person. Your face was radiant, and it still is. You've been light-hearted and just bubbling over all afternoon."

Ginger laughed lightly. "That's the way I feel," she admitted, "but I didn't know it showed."

"Darren Banning is bad news for any woman," Tina warned, "and especially one like you. I've seen him discard too many women in the nine years I've worked here. He won't marry you, and you're not the kind of girl to have an affair with him, so it won't take him long to cast you aside."

"Well, really," Ginger protested, "I'm not intending to marry the man."

"Take a good look at Maureen now that she knows he's getting tired of her," Tina continued, "and you'll see what I mean. All I'm saying is, be careful."

"Thanks, Tina, I'll be all right," Ginger assured her, but she knew that her friend's advice had come too late.

As Ginger read her Bible that evening, she knew that

she needed an answer to this new problem. Having watched Sally and Roger Stone for the past few months, Ginger had a new concept of the depth of feeling possible between man and woman. She knew that she loved Darren a great deal, but should she keep on seeing him? How long would he respect her Christian principles? What would happen when he tired of her? She was a novelty to him now, but, when he realized that she wouldn't bend her principles, would he drop her?

Lord, show me the answer, she prayed. *Why am I attracted to him? I've given my life to You, and I know I can't be happy for long with a man who denies You.*

Her Bible was open to the eighth chapter of Romans, and she glanced down at a passage that she had marked with a red pencil some time in the past. "And we know that all things work together for good to them that love God, to them who are called according to His purpose."

Did the message mean that God would bring some good out of their stormy relationship? She believed that that was God's answer, and, although she couldn't foresee the end result, she went about her work with more optimism than she had experienced for many days.

When the day of the rodeo dawned hot and clear, Ginger dressed with particular care, wearing khaki pants and jacket with a matching knit V-necked sweater. Not too dressy for a rodeo, she hoped.

When he arrived, he was attired in a white western hat, cowboy boots, a plaid shirt, form-fitting white denims, and a red neckerchief. She'd always heard of people who dress like "a million dollars," and who else had a better right to look that way!

"You look like a typical cowboy," she greeted him. "Are you riding in the rodeo?"

He laughed. "Hardly! But I had to dress appropriately. How do I look?"

"Wonderful!" she assured him.

"You look wonderful, too," he said, as he opened the door for her. "Have you been sewing again?"

"No, I bought this on sale."

As they headed westward, he smiled benignly, and said, "I hardly know how I was fortunate enough to have you for a whole day. No studies this weekend?"

"Oh, I have plenty of work I should be doing. But Ken and I didn't work at the gym today. I'll catch up when I get home tonight."

He frowned at her. "I'm not going to hurry home for you to study. The rodeo won't be over until late afternoon, and, I'm not hurrying back."

"Do you enjoy a rodeo so much that you don't want to miss any of it?"

"I like them well enough, but my main reason for choosing this rodeo was that I couldn't think of anyplace else you'd agree to go! I didn't think this would be too sinful for you. Although you may hear an occasional cussword." She glanced sideways to see if he were making fun of her, but his face didn't reveal his thoughts.

He switched on the car's stereo, and Ginger leaned back and enjoyed classical music. They were half-way to North Platte when he dropped a small box in her lap, saying, "That's a token to ask your forgiveness for the way I talked to you last week. I thought you might be getting tired of roses."

Ginger stared ahead. How could she get him to stop spending money on her? In distress she said, "I wish you wouldn't buy gifts for me."

"Why not?" he asked crossly.

"For one thing, I just don't like it."

He arched his eyebrows. "Are you afraid I'm going to try to collect for them sometime?"

She blushed a little, knowing what he meant by *collect*.

"Perhaps," she answered honestly.

She could tell that he was trying to check his anger, as he said, "You've already made it quite plain that you can't be bought, so forget that.

"But it just doesn't look right," Ginger protested. "Even if we aren't having an affair, people think we are when you buy expensive gifts for me. And you're wasting your money. Like that air conditioner, for instance. I tried to get the company to take it back, but I knew it would cause me more embarrassment if I made an issue of it. It's just sitting there unused."

He must have driven ten miles before he spoke again. White anger lines were etched around his mouth, and his dark mustache fairly bristled. When he did speak, she could tell that he was making a tremendous effort to be calm.

"Ginger, I was determined not to quarrel with you. I didn't want anything to spoil our day."

"I'm not quarreling, but you have to stop buying things for me. I don't know why you do it."

"I don't know why I do it either," he said, almost in wonder. "I can assure you it isn't habitual with me."

She looked at him quickly. "You mean you don't buy Maureen's jewelry?" Horrified that she had questioned him about his relationship with Maureen, she covered her flaming face and said, "I'm sorry. Just forget I said that."

He laughed heartily, reached across the seat and pulled her closer to him. "Well, Miss Prude, you've finally shown a human tendency—unpardonable curiosity about my personal affairs. For shame!" She could tell by his tone that he was teasing now, but she didn't answer.

"But, for your information, I've never bought Maureen any jewelry. She gets such a large salary that she's able to buy it herself. As a matter of fact, I've never bought jewelry for anyone except you. And that's the amazing thing! Many women have hounded me for favors, and I know they would lay claim to me if I bought them gifts. And here you are! You won't take anything from me, and I lavish gifts on you." He shook his head in amazement. "I suppose it's just plain stubbornness on my part."

She tried to digest that bit of information. Was she different from the others? Did he think more of her than some of his other conquests? If so, why?

"I bought that gift to ask your forgiveness. It isn't nearly as expensive as the other necklace, and surely didn't strain my finances." He placed his hand on her knee. "Please take it—there aren't any strings attached. If you wear it, I'll know you've forgiven the way I talked to you."

Ginger opened the box and her eyes bulged. Another diamond necklace! This one sported a precious stone set in a small golden triangle. Was he trying to put his "brand" on *her* with such a suggestive piece of jewelry?

"I bought it for you in New Orleans," Darren told her.

"Even when you were mad at me?"

"I wasn't nearly as mad at you as I was at myself. I feared I'd made such a mess of things that you'd be through with me."

Ginger couldn't make up her mind—should she take

it or not? Finally she said, "Thank you very much. I'll accept this, if you'll promise not to buy me anything else."

He laughed. "No deal. If I see something that I want to get for you, I'll buy it. I'll not have a little minx like you giving me orders."

"I can't keep you from buying things, but I don't have to accept them." She put on the necklace, and turned her back to him. "Be sure the catch is fastened. I don't want to lose it."

With her back turned, he took his eyes from the road for a moment and dropped a quick kiss on her neck. Goosebumps raced up and down her spine, and she faced him quickly. He drew her close and laughed softly. He was in a good humor now that he'd bent her will to his. He'd won a battle, Ginger conceded, but the war wasn't over yet.

The cheering crowd added excitement to the North Platte rodeo as the chute opened and a bucking horse bolted into the arena. The horse's body appeared in perpetual motion as the cowboy held on to the simple leather rigging. He stayed on the horse for ten seconds before tumbling off.

Once the bareback riding event was finished, the bulldogging contests started. Darren explained that this was the most dangerous part of the rodeo, for the cowboy had to jump from his running horse onto the steer's back, grab it by the horns, and wrestle it to the ground.

When the first rider completed his performance, he dashed away from the angry steer, whose attention was diverted by a clown who had jumped from a nearby barrel. The antagonized steer started chasing the clown, who kept the animal occupied until the cowboy reached the safety of the fence. Then, the clown, too, sprinted for cover.

"Oh," Ginger breathed in relief, "I thought he would catch the clown." Clowns had been evident throughout the rodeo, entertaining the crowd with their antics between the main attractions. The steer-wrestling continued without mishap, although Ginger sat spellbound every time until the clown and the cowboy had escaped from the angry steers.

Darren bought popcorn and Cokes from a passing vendor during intermission. "Having a good time, Miss Prude?" he asked fondly. With her mouthful of popcorn, all Ginger could do was nod. She assumed that "Miss Prude" was going to be her nickname from now on, but the tenderness in his voice robbed the word of any malice.

The cowgirls' barrel-racing was the last event of the day, and Ginger liked it best of all. "Each contestant has to run her horse in a cloverleaf pattern around those three large barrels," Darren explained. "They're timed on how long it takes to go through the pattern. If they knock over a barrel, the judges add five seconds to their total."

Darren took her hand to keep her close to him as they left the grandstand. How much fuller her life had been since she'd known him! In only a few times together, he had introduced her to many new things. Would it continue? Would the newness soon wear off?

As they neared the parking lot, someone yelled, "Hey, Banning!" Darren mumbled something underneath his breath and turned. "Now what?" he spat. "I drove two hundred miles to get away from people who knew me. I didn't want anyone to bother us today."

A middle-aged man detached himself from a small

group, and came toward them. "Howdy, Banning. What brings you out here?"

Darren shook hands with him. "How are you, Steve?" The man immediately turned to Ginger. "Steve, this is my friend, Ginger Wilson. Ginger, meet Mr. Lewis, president of a local bank." At least Darren wasn't ashamed of her, Ginger thought, for he still held her hand.

"Some of us are having dinner together, Banning. Why don't you and Miss Wilson join us?"

Ginger's spirits plummeted, but she brightened when Darren said, "Thanks, Steve, but we need to get back to Lincoln."

Steve Lewis insisted, but Darren still refused. "No, not today. You'll be coming to the meeting in Omaha next month, won't you? We'll get together then. Nice to see you, Steve."

"You bet," Lewis answered, as Darren hustled Ginger away.

"That was a narrow escape," Darren said. "I don't intend to share you with anyone today."

He opened the driver's door and let Ginger slide in. When she started to move to the far right, he caught her arm. "You stay over here. I get lonesome with you so far away." She did as he told her.

Slowly he manipulated the white Cadillac through the departing rodeo traffic and downtown North Platte until they reached the Interstate. Darren pulled her close, hugged her tightly with his free arm, and planted a hasty kiss on her forehead. "I like your company, Ginger. Thanks for coming with me."

Her throat ached to tell him how much she loved him, but caution won out. He was too dear to her, and she didn't want to scare him away. She did dare to lean her head on his shoulder and cuddle closer to him.

The way his arm tightened proved that he liked her response.

"Are you going to sleep on me again?" he asked quizzically.

"No, just resting...and thinking."

They'd been on the road for about an hour when he left the Interstate and drove into a park beside a small lake. "Let's stop awhile, Miss Prude. I'm tired of sitting, and I want to talk with you."

The area was almost deserted. They walked hand-in-hand until they came to a wooden bench facing the water. A cottonwood tree provided welcome shade from the late evening sun. Quietness was settling over the lake, broken occasionally by the croak of a bull frog. A pheasant crowed in a nearby field.

"It's peaceful here," Ginger said.

Darren stretched his legs out in front of him and took a deep breath. Ginger sat close to him with their shoulders touching.

"There's a big lake at the ranch," Darren told her. "Sometimes in the evening I go there and sit on the bank until it's dark. Sometimes I fish, but usually I just sit. I'd like for you to see it, Ginger."

What could she say to that? she wondered, and she didn't respond. He didn't appear to be in a talkative mood, even though he had said that he wanted to talk.

Soon, however, he turned to face her, and put his arm along the bench behind her. "Ginger, I don't want any misunderstanding between us."

She made no answer, but looked questioningly at him.

"Maureen is my secretary, and a good one," he went on. "If she weren't capable, I wouldn't keep her around for a day. There isn't anything else between us, nor have I ever given her reason to think there would be. She goes where I go because I'm always conducting business, even at lunch, and I need a record of what I say."

Ginger smiled. "A good tape recorder would cost much less."

"I suppose so, but there are also occasions, like dinners and some meetings, where a single man is out of place. If people are inclined to read something into our companionship, it doesn't matter to me. When I need a dinner partner, she's available. Do you believe me?"

She searched his eyes for several minutes. If she were any judge of character at all, then he was telling the truth. "Yes," she said softly.

"But I'll manage to get along without her outside of the office if it bothers you. And you can be assured that, as long as you let me see you, I won't be seeing any other woman. I'm not a two-timer, whatever my other faults may be. OK?"

She nodded, and the setting sun cast softening rays around them. "Then let me kiss you," he whispered.

"No," she protested, although her heart was willing. "I don't think we should."

He laughed at her. "Why not? A few kisses won't steal your virtue."

"I just don't want to get involved in an affair with you."

"Well, I want to get involved in an 'affair' with you," he returned. "You're affecting me like no woman I've ever known before, but I also know what kind of girl you are. I promise never to push my advances farther than you're willing to go. Isn't that fair enough?"

He cupped his hand behind her head, and, when he lowered his face to hers, she closed her eyes to avoid his eager gaze. His kiss was gentle, not demanding like the last time. The emotion rising in Ginger's breast almost smothered her, and she was sorry when he pulled away.

"Ginger," he whispered, "open your eyes and look at me." His eyes were dark with emotion. "Put your arms around my neck and kiss me. You aren't afraid now, are you?"

Ginger answered by slowly slipping her arms over his shoulders. As he slowly and gently caressed her hair and face, she responded with an intensity that surprised both of them. After a long kiss that left her breathless, his lips moved to her eyelids, then to the tips of her ears, her throat, and back to her lips again. Ginger molded her body close to his, and surrendered herself more fully to his embrace. Her body tingled, and she was consumed by a longing for fulfillment that she hungered for and feared at the same time.

I can't stand anymore of this, she thought, but, when he released her, she was disappointed. "Oh, Darren," she whispered, and reached up to brush back the hair from his forehead.

He laughed softly, and pulled her to him again. "I like that a lot better than 'Mr. Banning,' sweetheart."

She smiled and raised her lips, seeking his again. Ginger knew that she didn't have the strength to deny him anything.

Perhaps Darren knew it, too, for, after another long kiss, with his mustache gently caressing her face, he put her determinedly from him. "That's enough for now, Miss Prude. You learn fast."

She leaned her head on his shoulder, content now just to be near him.

"Do you know your hair turns golden in the twilight?"

She shook her head. "But don't get any idea of making one of your triangles out of it."

He pulled her upward, and said regretfully, "We'd better go. It will be late now before I get you home, and Mrs. Gainer will notice that."

Ginger wished that he hadn't mentioned Mrs. Gainer. It reminded her of the side of him that she wanted to forget.

When they got in the Cadillac, he sat her firmly beside him. "That is your seat when you're with me. If you don't stop trying to push out the right side of the car, we're going to use your little VW so you can't get far away."

As darkness settled down, only the light from the dashboard illuminated his face. He laid his hand on her knee and said, "Ginger, maybe I'd better say something else. I don't want to scare you away, but I should be honest with you."

She wondered what was coming, and she waited with tension mounting.

"I'm not the marrying kind, Ginger, and I think you should know that. I don't want you to think my attentions mean more than they do. *I won't marry you.*"

Grimacing, she turned her face to hide her disillusionment. "That's all right. I don't want to marry you either."

That silenced him momentarily. "You don't have to be so personal about it. I don't intend to marry *anyone*—I wasn't thinking of you in particular."

"Thanks for warning me. I didn't think I was the marrying kind either, but lately I've changed my mind about it."

"Who changed your mind? Ken?" he asked quickly.

She laughed and turned to look at him. "Are you jealous of Ken?"

"Yes, I think I am," he admitted surprisingly. "He's always underfoot, and evidently the things he has to offer mean more to you than what I have. You and he have more in common, that's obvious. I must seem an old man to you, but Ken is about your age. He goes to church, and apparently has the ethical principles that you think I lack. Besides, he's poor as a church mouse." He added, "All *I* have is several million dollars, but you've already made it plain that money means nothing to you."

She tugged at his ear and leaned over to kiss him on the cheek. "Ken Grady is just a friend."

"Friendship often blossoms into something more," he returned.

Maybe it will between you and me, she thought, but she said, "Well, I don't know about that. But Roger and Sally are the ones who've changed my attitude toward marriage. After my mother's bad marriage—the one I told you about—I didn't think anything could force me to get married. But, after being with Roger and Sally and seeing how they love Patrick, I'm beginning to think I'd like to have a family someday."

He turned to look at her intently.

"It won't be soon, I'm sure," Ginger said. "I want to earn my college degree first, but I wanted to be honest with you, too." She paused a moment. "I can't understand your viewpoint though. With all the wealth you've accumulated, I'd think you would want a family to pass it on to when you're dead. Wouldn't you like to have a son to carry on the Banning family name?"

A sudden stab of pain crossed his face, but he made no reply. The silence became pregnant with unuttered words. Somehow she had said the wrong thing.

Ginger was sorry to upset him, but she welcomed

the quiet to think about what had happened to her. His overtures had caught her by surprise this afternoon, and she'd been putty in his hands. He had known it, too, and she would be forever grateful that he'd used the restraint that she hadn't had.

She asked the Lord to forgive her for desiring Darren so strongly. She also prayed for courage to keep the strong-willed banker at arm's length from now on.

"Goodnight, Miss Prude," Darren whispered, when they had arrived at her doorway. "You've been the best sweetheart a man could ever want." His eyes sparkled as she reveled in the circle of his arm. He kissed her long and hard, but she suppressed her ardor. He must have sensed her constraint, for he looked at her keenly before he released her.

"I'm assuming that an 'affair' does exist between us now," he said smiling. "So may I call often?"

"As often as you can." She gently smoothed his mustache with the tip of her finger before she quickly turned to enter the trailer.

Ginger ran back and forth across the polished gym floor, trying to keep up with the excited players. How much she and Ken had accomplished with them in a few months!

The cheering spectators encouraged their favorite team as the gym resounded with the sounds of squeaking wheelchairs, excited athletes, and dribbling basketballs. With a sudden burst of energy, a paraplegic wheeled in between his teammates and threw the ball in to the lowered basket, giving his team the victory.

Parents and children cheered from the sidelines. Ginger kissed and hugged all of the participants, overjoyed to share this moment of accomplishment with those who had so many difficulties in life.

Amid their rejoicing, Ken touched her on the shoulder and motioned to the door of the gym. Darren was there, watching them. *How long has he been standing there?* she wondered. A white knit shirt and green shorts were convenient for refereeing a ball game, but she knew she looked tousled and flushed. As she ran to him, she brushed her hair with her hand.

He seemed oblivious to her appearance, but she was quick to notice the old look of unhappiness and desperation in his eyes. *What now?* she thought. He still was observing the group of children on the gym floor.

"I didn't know this was the type of children you were teaching," Darren said, with gritted teeth.

"I told you I was studying Special Education," Ginger reminded him.

He shook his head impatiently. "That didn't mean anything to me. Why did you choose such a profession, Ginger?"

She looked at the happy children, comparing this joyful moment to their apathy when she and Ken had started working with them. How could she explain the sense of achievement that she felt? "I have compassion for them," Ginger said slowly. "They need help, and so few people love them."

"And you're always interested in the underdog, aren't you?"

She was hurt by his words and tone. "I don't know that it's a bad characteristic to have," she said kindly.

"I came to get you. Sally said you'd driven with Ken. Are you ready to go home?"

"Usually we leave around noon, but not today. This is our last meeting for the term, and we're taking the children on a picnic. It'll be late when I'm finished. But my summer classes are over now, and I'll have lots of free time for a month."

Darren frowned. "That won't do me any good. I'm eaving for Texas tonight."

"When will you come back?" she asked, trying to hide her disappointment.

"I don't know," he said shortly.

"Why not come with us this afternoon? We could use some extra help."

"You must be out of your mind," he retorted. "You can spend time with the degenerates of society if you like, but I can think of less revolting company."

"Why, Darren!" she cried, hardly believing that she'd heard him correctly.

"I'm sorry, Ginger, but you might as well know how I feel. I can't stand to be around the handicapped. They're repulsive to me."

How dare he feel that way! she thought, as he stalked away. *When God has given him the best of everything—a superb body and superior intellect, as well as a fortune, how can he be so unfeeling toward these unfortunate people?*

She was so angry with him that she wanted to run after him and strike him. But, as he strode out of sight, without a backward glance, her anger turned to sorrow and despair. She had detected still another flaw in his character, when all she had wanted to see was perfection.

Chapter Six

Persistent ringing awakened Ginger, and she sleepily reached a hand from under the covers to shut off the alarm. *Why did I set the alarm on my first day of vacation?* she wondered. The clock face showed nine o'clock, but she realized as her hand felt the alarm button, that it was the *doorbell* which she heard. She waited, hoping the caller would leave, but the ringing continued. Putting on a robe, she hurried into the living room.

Smiling broadly, Darren entered as soon as she unlocked the door. "Hello, sweetheart," he said. "What an unexpected pleasure to see how you look when you get up in the morning!" He enveloped her in a bear hug and kissed her eagerly. She hadn't seen him since that day at the gym.

She tied the robe securely when he released her, conscious of how revealingly thin her summer garments were, and that Darren was observing her with obvious delight.

"I returned last night, and found out this morning that you have a week's vacation. Pack your clothes. We're going to the ranch!"

Startled, Ginger shook her head. "You know I can't go with you."

"You don't have any classes; you told me that. You have a free week. What had you planned to do?"

"Some sewing and cleaning my home."

"Some vacation!" he retorted. "Come on, get ready."

How she wanted to go with him! The more he had talked about his ranch, the more she'd wanted to see it. But it was impossible.

When she hesitated, he said, "And if you're worried about your reputation, Ike and Melissa can stay in the house with us. They'll hear you call if you need protection from me."

She was weakening, but she didn't want him to know. "I'm not afraid of you."

"Good. Get ready to go."

"What will people say?" Ginger asked.

"I don't care, Miss Prude. Anyway, how many people would even know where you are?"

"I won't go away without telling Sally. She would worry."

He nodded and picked up the telephone receiver. He gave a credit card number, and then waited. Soon he said, "Melissa, I want to bring my friend, Ginger Wilson, up to the ranch this week, but she's a nice girl and won't come unless she's properly chaperoned. Will you tell her it's safe?" He handed the phone to Ginger.

Melissa spoke in a kind voice. "Miss Wilson, I'm always in the house during the daytime, and we can stay at night too if you want to come. I'd *like* to see Mr. Banning bring a nice girl home with him. We'd love to have you."

Ginger wondered how many "bad" girls he'd taken

96

to the ranch. "All right." She said to Melissa, "Under those conditions, I'll be happy to come."

Darren gave her a quick kiss before he took the receiver. "We'll be there in time for dinner," he assured Melissa. His pleasure was almost boyish, and Ginger shared his excitement.

"I'll give you a half-hour to get ready," he said.

"You'll give me more time than that, or I won't go. I have to shower and wash my hair, besides packing. And I haven't had any breakfast."

"Neither have I, so I'll prepare something to eat while you get ready."

"How are we going?" Ginger asked.

"We're flying, of course," he declared as she hurried down the hall. Ginger never had flown in a plane. What an exciting life Darren lived!

"What kind of clothes should I take?" she called as she pulled a suitcase from the closet. "What will we be doing?"

"I'll be working part of the time, and you can do anything you want to then. But we'll ride horseback, hike, fish…"

"Then I won't need any dress-up clothes?"

"Yes, you will. I want you to look pretty for me. And take a swimsuit, too. I have a pool."

"I don't have a swimsuit. You know I can't swim."

Ginger chose two of her prettiest dresses. She darted into the living room and got her knitting bag to put in the luggage.

Ginger was breathless by the time they finally were on their way. When they got to the highway, Darren turned the white Cadillac toward Lincoln instead of going to the airport. Ginger looked at him questioningly and he grinned. "I'm going to buy you a swimsuit!"

"No," she said, but he ignored her. They still hadn't reached an agreement about gifts. Every time he went somewhere, he brought her a gift, which she always laid aside and refused to use.

He had brought her several yards of Scottish woolen fabric when he had come back from Canada. Upon his return from Mexico, he had presented Ginger with two silver bud vases and a hand-tooled, leather purse. After his New York trip, he had given her the largest bottle of Chanel No. 5 perfume that she'd ever seen. All of the unused gifts were on a table in her living room. He didn't mention them, and neither did she.

Darren drove into the first shopping center and asked, "What size do you wear?"

"Darren, I wish you wouldn't!"

He opened the door, "You might as well tell me. I'll get one anyway, and I'd like for it to fit."

Exhaling, she said, "Either a 34, or a 10, depending on how they're sized." As he walked away, she lowered the window. "And don't get a bikini. I won't wear it." He merely waved at her.

Upon his return, he threw a package into her lap. "I bought two to give you a choice. And I also got you a beach robe for covering, Miss Prude."

As he sped along the Interstate, Ginger asked, "What time does the plane leave?"

"Whenever I get ready."

She laughed. "Oh, come now, Darren. I know you're important, but not so much so that a whole airline will wait for you. Or do you own Frontier Lines, too?"

He looked at her oddly. "We're going in my plane. Didn't you know I owned one?"

Her eyes widened. "You mean you're the pilot?"

"Sure. You aren't afraid to travel with me, are you?"

"Of course not," she answered. "I'm just surprised, that's all. Do you go in your own plane on all these trips you take?"

"Most of the time, unless I'm going out of the United States. Then I take a commercial flight."

His plane was a four-passenger Beechcraft. It was white, of course, with golden triangles on the wings. Ginger was a bit nervous as they waited on the runway for flight instructions, but he flashed her a reassuring smile as he talked with the control tower. Her mood changed to exhilaration as he guided the plane down the runway and smoothly into the sky. She might have known that he was a good pilot, too.

Oh, darling, she thought, *I love you*. Why couldn't his business practices and moral principles be more compatible with her beliefs? She wanted him forever, but their relationship always seemed to hang by a thread.

Once in the air, Darren set the cruising speed at 100 mph, and he pointed out landmarks to her. Ginger looked down at the broad checkerboard of fields, with their sections of wheat stubble, alfalfa fields, and corn. Large irrigation pivots moved back and forth across the fields.

After they left central Nebraska, the farms disappeared, and they flew over rangelands, dotted by large lakes. Darren dropped in altitude, so that she might see the country better. Flying for many miles without sighting any towns or habitations, he finally said excitedly, "We've just crossed the border of my ranch." He was as exuberant as a boy showing off his favorite toy.

Cattle dotted the range, and Ginger said, "All of the cattle are white!"

"That's right, and the horses are too. I sold all the

other kinds of animals a few years ago."

"A white car, white plane, and now white live-stock!"

He tugged playfully at her hair. "And I may just have you bleach that red hair, too. It doesn't fit in with the rest of my decor."

She glanced quickly at him, remembering Maureen's blond tresses. "Don't you like my hair?"

"Darling, I was only joking. I like you just the way you are." He pointed to a group of buildings. "There are the ranch headquarters. All white, too, except the house. It's built of Colorado granite; I wanted it to blend in with the hues of the land." He circled low over a large field to the right of the buildings. A long structure had "Golden Triangle Ranch" printed in large yellow letters on its roof, and Ginger assumed that the paved runway was his private landing strip.

"Are you still buckled in?" he asked. "We're about to land."

Soon Darren taxied the plane into the hangar and unlocked a nearby garage, where a white pickup truck was stored. He helped her into the high seat of the cab. "You're a rancher up here, Miss Prude, so no Cadillacs. Either a pickup or a horse will be your mode of trans-portation." He stood between the open door of the truck and her seat and drew her close to him. "I ha-ven't had a kiss for half-a-day, and I'd better get one before Melissa starts watching us."

Darren's hands moved to her back and his lips met hers. His eyes were dark with passion when he lifted his head and smoothed back her hair. Planting a kiss on her forehead, he murmured "I'm never really sure of you, Ginger, unless I have you in my arms." Apparently she had kept him unaware of her deep feeling for him. Did he really care if he lost her?

100

Her fingers traced his chin, the neat mustache, his nose, and the arched eyebrows. *Lord, you can change him into the kind of person he should be. You promised that all things work together for good*, she prayed silently.

"I said you suited me as you are," Darren was saying, "but there is one thing I wish was different."

"I told you weeks ago that I wouldn't change, but I'm curious to know what you'd alter if you could," she said with a smile, still secure in the circle of his arms.

"I keep wanting more from you than I ever get," he answered. "You're always holding back, keeping me at arm's length. I want you to be warm and eager like you were that day under the cottonwood tree." So he had noticed her reserve!

"That was my first experience with that kind of closeness and yearning, and I was taken by surprise. I learned then how easy it would be to get carried away and do something I'd be ashamed of the rest of my life. You promised that I could call a halt to our emotions, and I have to do that."

"And I'm keeping that promise," he said grimly, "but it's the hardest job I've ever had."

"I'm having a fight with my conscience, anyway," Ginger continued seriously. "I'm doubtful that I should even allow you to kiss and hold me the way you do."

"Forget I said anything," he said quickly. "I'd rather have part of you than nothing. But you trouble me, Ginger. I'm miserable when I'm away from you, but I'm trying to consolidate my business interests, so I won't have to travel so much. Before I met you, I didn't care where I was, but now I want to be where I can keep my eye on you." Giving her thigh a swat with his hand, he closed the door, went to the driver's side and backed the vehicle of the garage.

Darren's ranch house was protected by a sheltering belt of evergreens, and Ginger didn't see his home until they were almost upon it. Built on a slope, the residence seemed to have sprouted from the ground. They cleared the green band of trees and approached from the rear which had two floors, while the front half of the house was only one story.

Darren drove into a carport that was occupied by a white van. "We use that when the weather is too bad to haul supplies in the pickup," he explained.

They entered through the back, greeted Melissa, a matronly woman in her late fifties, and then toured the house. The kitchen and the dining room were on the second level, over the garage, and a large deck extended beyond the dining room.

A spacious, tree-lined courtyard—with a triangle-shaped swimming pool—separated the kitchen area from the rest of the house. Access to the living quarters was gained through a hallway lined with statuary and greenery. Sliding glass doors offered frequent passage to the courtyard, where, in one corner, water cascaded in a marble fountain.

The front porch overlooked a neatly-kept, spacious lawn that spread to the lake far below. White ducks and geese added beauty to the lake. White cattle dotted the green pastures in the distance.

The living room had a cathedral ceiling, and was furnished lavishly with comfortable couches and chairs. The living and bedroom areas were carpeted in white, and the golden triangle motif was evident somewhere in every room. Nothing was out of place—the whole house was immaculate.

Ginger's quarters were evidently designed for a lady.

Ruffled curtains, bedspread, and pillow shams, and the canopied bed cover all were a delicate blue. The almond-colored furniture was daintier than furnishings in the other rooms. The bathroom fixtures were white marble, and the circular tub was installed at floor level, with two steps leading to the water. She noted four other guest rooms besides this one.

Darren's rooms were on the same level as the garage. He showed her his large office, and a bedroom containing a king-sized bed and other massive furniture. Adjoining was a recreation room which was larger than her mobile home! The room sported a pool table, and, at the opposite end, a bar, behind which were a stove and refrigerator. Leather furniture was grouped in the middle of the room before a big television, and one side of the room was lined with shelves full of books and videotapes.

Outside the recreation room was a patio, where stone tables and benches, as well as a gas grill, were installed. "We'll have dinner out there some evening," Darren promised.

Ginger dressed with care for dinner that evening, wearing a sundress of white eyelet, with slender straps over the shoulders. She put on a short-sleeved jacket, and, as a final touch, she hung his diamond pendant around her neck.

Darren was waiting for her on the deck, and after appraising her, he said teasingly, "Take off the jacket, Miss Prude. There's no one to see except me." He removed her jacket, and she stiffened when he kissed both of her shoulders, but he promised, "I'll be good."

Ginger was awed at the splendor of the dining table, set with expensive china, crystal, and sterling silver.

The whole room seemed to sparkle, and she wondered if Darren ever denied himself anything.

Once the meal was placed on the buffet, Melissa left them to serve themselves. Darren smiled fondly at Ginger and said, "You can offer thanks, if you want to. I always notice when you bow your head before we eat in a restaurant." She reached gratefully for his hand, and he clasped hers tightly, while she thanked God for the safety of their journey, as well as for the food they were to eat.

The meal was delightful—herbed chicken with rice, glazed carrots, minted green peas, and a vegetable salad. The hot rolls were freshly baked, and, for dessert, Melissa brought them cherry pie à la mode.

"I don't know how you stay so slender," Ginger said, "if she cooks like this all of the time."

"Remember, I'm not up here very much."

After dinner, they sat outside on the deck in a large padded chaise lounge that was big enough to accommodate both of them. He talked about the first years that he had had the ranch, and how he had accumulated his vast holdings.

Melissa came out when her work was done. "Miss Wilson," she said, "I'll be sleeping across the court from you." And to Darren, "Ike called, and he'll be late getting home. Probably he won't see you until morning."

Ginger snuggled closer to Darren as the night air brought coolness. She put her arms around his waist, her head on his shoulder. He held her close, and she almost went to sleep in his arms, until he shook her a little.

"You'd better go to bed, Ginger. Tomorrow we'll start enjoying your vacation."

"I've enjoyed today," she murmured. "Thanks for bringing me, Darren."

He walked with her to her bedroom, switched on the lights, and checked the room. He unlatched a sliding door and showed her a small balcony. Suddenly he bent to kiss her lips, and then turned and left the room abruptly. Ginger smiled a little, comprehending slightly what a difficult fight he was having with himself.

She stood by the door into the hall after he left, her hand on the lock. Should she lock herself in? She decided against it. She wasn't going to mistrust him now.

In the strange surroundings, Ginger found it hard to go to sleep. *Had he brought other women here?* Even though he had said there was nothing between him and Maureen, she knew that he must have been involved with other women. And the room had been used. She had discovered a small cigarette burn on the white carpet, and a crack in the lavatory where some heavy object had been dropped. Putting thoughts of his conquests out of her mind, she turned under the blue coverlet and finally went to sleep.

The sound of the door opening awakened her. She cautiously raised her head. The door closed again, and she saw a note leaning on the table beside the door. She jumped out of bed to read his message.

It said, "Good morning, Sweetheart! Ike and I have some work to do for a few hours. My home is yours, so do what you want. We'll spend the afternoon together. DB."

She stayed in bed until she heard horses and riders outside. Donning a robe, she went out on the balcony. Darren and another man were riding by, but Darren saw her and waved. She threw him a kiss, and, even at a distance, she saw the flash of his delighted smile. She thrilled at Darren's easy grace on the horse.

The phone at her bedside rang, and Melissa asked, "Miss Wilson, would you like to have your breakfast served in bed?"

"Oh, no, Melissa. You don't have to bother. I'm used to taking care of myself."

"Mr. Banning said to serve you this morning. If you're up, I'll bring it in."

Ginger asked Melissa to put the breakfast tray on the balcony table. "I appreciate this, Melissa, but don't do it anymore. I don't want to make any extra work for you."

"No trouble at all, Miss. I like having company."

"Aren't there any other women here?"

"Several of the ranch workers are married, and I see their wives occasionally. I have a sister and children in Scotts Bluff, and we go there a lot when Mr. Banning is away."

Ginger spent the morning walking on the grounds, and then down to the lake. When she returned, she took her knitting to the deck and waited for Darren to return. His eyes glowed at the sight of her. "What a domestic scene! I thought I told you no working this week."

She laid the knitting aside and rose to greet him. "I'm making Patrick a sweater, and I want to get it finished before fall classes start. Besides, I'm not in the habit of obeying you."

Only the time that they had fallen in the Platte River had she seen him as disheveled and dirty as he was now. He waved her away when she approached him. He smelled like the stables, and he hadn't even shaved. "I'm too dirty to touch you now. Give me thirty minutes to shower and dress, and for the rest of the day I'm all yours."

"Have you done much horseback riding?" Darren asked as they strolled to the corral after lunch.

"A little, and I'm not afraid of horses. If you have a gentle one, I'll be all right."

Several men were working around the buildings, but Darren introduced her to only one. The small man was repairing a saddle, as they walked up. "Ginger, this is Ike Clark, the ranch manager. Ike, see if you can find a saddle for Miss Wilson, and choose a mount for her. We'll be riding quite a lot this week."

About thirty horses were grazing in the corral. Ginger climbed up on the wooden fence and exclaimed, "Why, Darren, you don't have all white animals— there's a black pony in there!" An old, shaggy pony was moping among the spirited white horses.

Darren didn't look at her, and his voice was expressionless. "We had Blacky before I switched to only one breed and color of horses. I've never bothered to get rid of him."

She knew well enough when Darren was withholding information. But the pony wasn't any of her business, and, when he wanted to tell her something, he would, and not before.

In consideration of her lack of experience, Darren rode leisurely, and pointed to his holdings with obvious pride. The area was like nothing Ginger had seen in Nebraska. The Sand Hills, sand dunes held in place by lush grasses, were a product of Ice Age droughts. Clusters of grayish-green yarrows and goldenrod bloomed. In areas where the sand had been blown about and moved by wind and cattle, sharp-bladed yucca stood tall against the whistling wind.

Pools of water supplied by natural underground reservoirs dotted the valleys between the towering sand ridges. White ducks and black-and-white willets nested on the lakes.

On one high dune, Darren stopped, and, with a sweep of his arm, indicated the surrounding countryside. "This is my favorite spot on the ranch. It's all mine, in every direction you look."

Ginger gazed long at the beautiful landscape with its hundreds of white cattle. "God said, 'for every beast of the forest is *mine*, and the cattle upon a thousand hills.' "

He frowned at her and said angrily, "*These* happen to be *mine*, Ginger. I've done it all myself, and I'll not give credit to God or anyone else."

Ginger didn't want to argue with him, but she said softly, "I can't help but wonder how much you'd have if the Lord hadn't given you the water, the sun, and the fertile land, as well as your healthy body and keen mind. No man is sufficient unto himself, Darren."

He jerked the reins of his horse and started off. She followed, sorry that she'd said anything, and realizing that he had brought her to the place so she would appreciate the immensity of his holdings. It rankled him that she wasn't impressed with his many worldly possessions.

After a few miles, he dropped back to ride with her again, having won a battle with his anger. Within a few miles of the ranch headquarters, she saw a group of buildings to the west. When she inquired about them, he said, "That's where the ranch hands live."

"Aren't we going over there?"

"No, there's nothing to see," he said shortly. "I want to get back in time for a swim before dinner. It's time for your first lesson."

She walked stiffly to the house, after the unaccustomed hours in the saddle! "I don't think I'm going swimming," she said.

He stopped and looked at her. "Why not?"

She wouldn't meet his gaze, but stood with eyes downcast, raking her shoe back and forth in the dust at her feet.

"Have you tried on your swimsuits?" he asked.

"No, but I've looked at them, and they're indecent."

"Well, I'm sorry, Miss Prude, but they don't manufacture Gay Nineties outfits anymore. Those two suits cover more than anything else I could find in that store." He lifted her head. "Tell me where the Bible says you shouldn't go swimming."

"You know there isn't anything about swimming in the Bible, but Grandmother wouldn't let me go swimming because she said modern swimsuits cause men to lust after the flesh. I just feel uncomfortable when I'm that near-naked."

He pulled off the big hat he'd loaned her, rumpled her hair, and laughed. "It's not 'lusting after the flesh' for me to teach you to swim. You should know how to swim for your own protection. Besides, it's good exercise."

"You wouldn't want me going swimming with any other man in such skimpy suits, would you?"

"Why not? There's nothing indecent about the human body." He patted her playfully on the fanny when they were climbing the steps to the deck. "I'm expecting you at the pool in a half-hour, properly attired."

Ginger inspected the bathing suits and wondered which one was the lesser of the two evils. If these were the least revealing he could find, she couldn't imagine how brief some of the others must have been!

One was a jade-colored maillot with a softly-shirred

double-keyhole front, elastized topline, and halter-tie straps.

The other swimsuit was fashioned of purple and beige mitered stripes with a low V-neck, scooped back, and high-cut legs. Noting that it tied twice in the back, she finally decided that she would be a little more secure in it.

She blushed when she put on the suit before the full-length mirror. Although she didn't have the voluptuous shape of Maureen Rowley, she had no reason to be ashamed of her appearance. Her breasts were firm and erect, even in this unlined swimsuit. Her stomach was flat, her hips were curved sensuously, and her legs were well-shaped. She was small, but nothing about her was skinny. She slipped on the hooded mini-robe of woven mesh with elastic wrists, and tied the rope belt.

Darren was swimming the length of the triangular pool when Ginger came out and sat timidly on the edge of a chair. When he climbed out of the pool, she dropped her gaze in embarrassment. *My word*, she thought, *he might as well be naked*! His knit briefs left nothing to the imagination.

He didn't spare her by ignoring her discomfiture. "I can't swim in my jeans, and I usually don't have an audience when I swim," he explained. He tugged at her robe. "Come on, let's see how you look." She let him untie the belt, and stood up as he slipped the robe off her shoulders. He stared at her in obvious appreciation, and Ginger felt her face burning. His silence was causing her more and more discomfort. Finally he said softly, "I've changed my mind about two things."

She glanced up questioningly. "First of all," Darren said, "I don't want you to go swimming with another man. And you may be right about 'lusting after the flesh.' "

She grabbed the robe and started back to the house. "I won't stay," she declared.

He caught her arm. "Yes, you will. You can't stop my thoughts, but I'll keep them to myself."

For the next hour, he gave her swimming instructions, accomplishing little except to give her enough confidence to float a bit. While he swam back and forth across the pool for a half-hour, Ginger floated on a tube and watched.

She had never spent such a miserable hour, and hoped that she'd concealed her sensations from him. His hands on her body while he had instructed her had been pure torture. Even a glance at his lithe body had caused her to tingle all over. Ginger was sorry that she'd ever agreed to come swimming, for she now had new problems to plague her.

"Miss Wilson," Melissa began, as Ginger helped clear away the luncheon dishes on Wednesday. "Do you mind if I leave for a few hours this afternoon? I know I promised you I'd be here, but my daughter is ill, and I'd like to go see her."

Ginger was afraid to be in the house alone with Darren after her titillating experience with him yesterday, but how could she say that to Melissa? "Go ahead, if you must, and don't worry about getting back before dinner. I can serve our meal."

Melissa showed Ginger where to find the food she had prepared, and said, "I'll be back before bedtime." *But it's ten hours until bedtime*, Ginger thought.

Ginger was in her room when she heard Ike and Melissa drive away, and the house had a strange feeling of emptiness, almost a foreboding. Soon Darren knocked

111

on her door. "Time for another swimming lesson," he called. "Come on out."

Should she feign illness and stay in her room? No, deceit wasn't part of Ginger's make-up, so she donned the other swimsuit and went to him. Perhaps Darren, too, was conscious that they were alone, for he made no remarks about her appearance, and worked impersonally with her in the water until she wearied from the exertion.

She stretched out in a lounge. The sun felt revitalizing on her wet body, and she decided to wait until he'd almost finished his vigorous swimming before she put on the robe. The gentle splashing of the water as it tumbled down the sides of the fountain lulled her to sleep.

She was awakened by the sound of his voice. "Scoot over a little." She moved reluctantly, and he lay on his side facing her. He closed his eyes, breathing deeply from the exercise. *I should get up*, Ginger thought. His eyes were on a level with hers, and, when he opened them, she saw the longing mirrored there. She'd waited too late to leave him.

He put his arms around her, and kissed her wet hair, her eyes, her nose, her ears. He claimed her lips last of all. It was a gentle kiss at first, but his caresses grew more passionate, and Ginger was aware of the violent ardor that she was stirring within him. He released her lips and dropped his head to her shoulder. She sensed that he was struggling for control, but his lips met hers again in a deep, suffocating kiss, and, with an audible moan, she slipped her arms around his neck. Time stood still.

When Ginger came to her senses, her eyes flew open and looked straight into his, which were now volcanic lakes of passion. With a strength she didn't know she possessed, Ginger broke their embrace and jumped off the lounge.

He reached for her. "Darling," he pleaded, "don't leave now. You were being so sweet."

"Darren, this is crazy. I'm going to my room."

He took possession of her arm. "No," he said.

"You promised!" She jerked away from him and stepped backward—into the deep end of the pool, narrowly missing the diving board as she fell! She screamed as the waters closed over her. He was in the pool with her immediately, and pulled her to safety, but the near tragedy had cooled their ardor.

Ginger glanced timidly at him, sitting beside her on the edge of the pool. He sat with head down. Was he angry with her? she wondered. At last, as if the past ten minutes had never happened, Darren said wearily, "Come on, Miss Prude, let's teach you to swim. I'm not always going to be around when you need to be fished out of the water."

He was very gentle with her for the rest of the afternoon.

"Ike and I have to go to Thedford this afternoon for supplies," Darren told her at lunch on Thursday. "You can go with us if you like."

"Will it be all right if I go riding instead?"

"Certainly; do what you like. We'll saddle your horse and leave it in the stable. There's nothing to hurt you, but I wouldn't go too far from home."

Ginger faced the afternoon with anticipation. The week was going too fast, and she already was dreading the time when they would have to leave. She intended to enjoy the rest of her vacation to the fullest, for, after that episode at the pool yesterday, she knew that the time was coming when she would have to stop seeing

Darren. Now that she knew the depth of passion they could reach, she was afraid of what might happen.

The old pony, Blacky, came to the fence, and stuck his nose through as she rode by. Why had Darren kept the animal?

She daydreamed as she rode slowly along the road. If circumstances were different, she would like to stay here all the time. The ranch appealed to her. She felt more at home here than at any other place she'd known. She had been welcome at her grandmother's, she knew, but it wasn't really *her* home.

"I want to marry him," she whispered aloud. "I love him, but he doesn't love me apparently. He says he doesn't want to lose me, but he only wants my body, and he won't even marry me for that! And I couldn't marry him anyway, when he's so cynical about my religious faith." What could the future hold for them?

Ginger's mount had been frisking along without any direction, and she suddenly found herself in the midst of a little settlement. Ginger looked about in surprise, hardly believing what was before her eyes. She was in the area where Darren's ranch families lived—and she blushed with shame at the comparison between their meager homes and the fabulous ranch house.

Why, the stables and barns for his horses are mansions compared to these hovels! Ginger had never been in the midst of such squalor, and she looked in disbelief as her horse pranced without guidance throughout the area. The half-dozen houses, scattered over a two- or three-acre plot, were one-story rickety frame buildings that had never seen a paintbrush. Apparently, no plumbing was available, for an outdoor privy was evident behind each house, and, in the midst of the neighborhood, a squeaking windmill pumped water into an overflowing tank. Water running from the tank created a mudhole around it. Hardly a blade of grass was to be seen, and Ginger's horse stirred up dust as they moved along. Tin cans and other debris were scattered throughout.

However, she noted television antennas sprouting from every roof. A motorcycle, seemingly new, stood before one house, but the other forms of transportation were decrepit cars and trucks.

At the last house, some children playing in the dirt looked up warily at her approach. She dismounted and greeted them. "Hello, I'm Ginger, and I'm staying over at Mr. Banning's. May I visit with you awhile?"

The older of the children, a boy about ten years old, nodded. "Sure. We're playing ball. Do you want to play with us?"

Their "ball" was nothing but a wad of rags sewn together. Ginger joined the ball game, but her mind wasn't on the playing. She was seething inside, as she thought about all of Darren's money, and wondered how he could be so stingy with those who worked for him.

The boy, whose name was Timmy, motioned to the house, and said, "There's my Mom, if you want to talk to her." Ginger approached the ramshackle house, and held out her hand to the blonde woman standing there. A little girl about Patrick's age held on to her mother's legs.

Ginger said, "Pardon me for intruding, but I was riding and stopped to play with the children."

"I'm Mildred Pederman. Come in, if you'd like."

The inside of the dismal house was devoid of much furniture. A color television dominated one corner of the room, but the other furnishings were old and worn. Ginger held the little girl, Ruth, on her lap.

Mildred said that her family only had been on the

ranch for a year. "My brother Jeff worked for Mr. Banning, and, when the plant closed where my husband was employed, we came here. We aren't very happy, but at least we can eat. My husband is proud, and he didn't want to accept welfare. I hated to take Timmy out of school, though."

"Don't these children go to school?"

"No. There's no school close by, and we can't afford to drive back and forth to Thedford each day. And I won't leave my children with anyone else, just so they can attend school."

"How many children live here?" Ginger asked.

"About a dozen of school age, I'd imagine."

The nerve of him, to deprive these children of an education! She supposed she was being unreasonable to expect him to build a school, but he should be humanitarian enough to do *something!* Of course, state laws dictated school attendance, but somehow, these children, whose families were probably transients, had escaped official notice.

Ginger went outside to play with the children, and the group had increased to fifteen kids of all ages. She couldn't stand the sight of the make-believe ball, and she taught them new games.

She led them in exercises—push-ups, leg-lifting, arm-swinging, walking and marching in place. They enjoyed some easy running games in which the smallest children could participate. Mildred watched fondly from the porch, and some of the other mothers joined her to view the newcomer among them.

They were running a sack race, using two old feed bags, when the white pickup truck drove into the yard. Darren got out. "What are you doing here, Ginger?" he demanded.

She was conscious of the dust on her face, hands,

116

jeans, and shirt. She was filthy. "You told me I could go where I wanted," she reminded him. She was angry, and wasn't about to be cowed by his obvious displeasure.

"You certainly are a mess. Get in the truck and come home with me," he ordered. "Ike here can bring your horse."

"No," she returned. "I'm not ready to leave yet." The muscles in his face twitched angrily, but he didn't say anything else in front of the gaping audience. Ike seemed amused that she dared to cross Darren.

She dallied for another hour after he left, and then rode slowly home, dreading the encounter with him.

When she climbed the steps to the deck—hot, dirty, and disheveled—he was lying on a lounge, immaculately dressed in white. He held a book, but she doubted he'd been reading.

"Melissa will have dinner in a half-hour," he said gruffly.

She didn't answer, but her piercing look caused him to lower his gaze as she went on to her room. She had a notion to go to supper in her dirty clothes just to spite him, but she didn't want to remain uncomfortable herself.

While she dressed, she compared her luxurious room, which was rarely used, to the poor habitations she'd seen this afternoon. *How could Darren be so unconcerned about the plight of others?* she wondered as she soaked in the luxury of the tub. She hurriedly shampooed and dried her hair, and dressed in a shorts set of classic gray sweatshirt fabric. The raglan sleeves and pockets were sparked with pink topstitching, and the collar, cuffs, and hem were made of pink polyester cotton knit. She wore a pair of canvas sneakers.

Her afternoon's experience wasn't mentioned during the meal, for he talked of what he and Ike had done during the day. When they went to the deck, he drew her down beside him, but her body was stiff and unyielding when he tried to embrace her.

"You're mighty quiet this evening," he said at last. "What's on your mind? You might as well say it."

"I can't imagine how you can lead the lifestyle you do, live in a mansion like this, and let your employees live in hovels," she blurted out.

He angrily left the chair, and walked away from her to look out over the lake. With an impatient gesture, he said, "Leave it alone, Ginger! We were having such a good time. Why did you have to go over there today? I brought you up here to enjoy yourself, not to meddle in my business."

"It's just like Mrs. Gainer's stock," she continued. "When you have so much, why do you begrudge something to others? You're selfish—you want everything for yourself."

He turned toward her. "By..." He caught himself in the midst of the oath, and Ginger remembered that he hadn't taken God's name in vain for weeks. "That's a lie, and you know it. I've wanted to give *you* enough that you won't accept."

"But that's for your own gratification. You know I don't want your gifts."

"Do you want me to give everything away, so I'll be penniless? Would that make you happy?"

"I'd like to see you happy, that's the point. With all you have, you still aren't happy."

He thrust his hands in his pockets, and stood silently for several minutes. Then he came and sat beside her, took her hand, and spoke as if he were talking to a child.

"You just don't understand business, sweetheart," he began. "Let's consider these people. Supposing that I turned this whole ranch over to them today. What do you think they'd do with it? First of all, they'd never do another day's work until it was all gone. They'd invite all their relatives to a feast, and what cows they didn't kill and eat, they'd sell to buy beer and whiskey. They'd live in this house, and in a few weeks it would be a shambles. They'd chop down the shrubbery to burn, and throw tin cans all over the lawn. I can't see any point in providing them with better houses, when they make a garbage heap of what I do furnish them."

She realized that there was probably some truth in his reasoning. "That may be," Ginger agreed. "They have to be taught frugality and how to amount to something."

"I pay them more money than they could get elsewhere. And if I didn't employ them, they'd be worse off than they are."

"But the children! Do you know what they were playing with—a ball made out of rags. I didn't see one toy around that whole area; nothing but dirt and squalor."

"But you did see all those fancy TV's, didn't you, and that expensive cycle? And if you'd looked in the kitchen, I bet you would have found expensive, pre-pared foods that they buy, rather than cooking decent food the way you and Melissa do. It isn't that they don't have any money—they *waste* what I pay them."

"Another generation will grow up the same way if those children don't go to school. You have a duty to those who work for you, Darren."

He whirled away from her again. "They don't stay in one place long enough to go to school. You don't know what you're talking about, so stay out of it."

"Besides, I'm concerned about you as much as the ranch workers."

"I don't need your concern," he retorted.

"You have your priorities all wrong," she continued. "Since you've made all your money in such a short time, the Lord obviously has given you a special talent for making money. That's a rare talent, and you should use it to help others. If you'd start sharing your possessions in a God-directed way, you couldn't live long enough to give away all the money you'd have! You can't outgive God."

He smiled coldly. "That's a lot of foolishness."

"You should be like the people mentioned in the New Testament who gave generously to help others," Ginger persisted, "after they gave *themselves* to *God*." She went to him, and put her arms around his waist, speaking earnestly, "I don't mean to meddle. I want to see you become a really big man."

"I *am* a big man," and he added bitterly, "to everyone but you."

"And God," she said softly.

He seemed surprised at her answer, but he growled, "I'm just the way I am, and you might as well get used to me that way. I won't change."

They were at the same impasse as usual. Both of them firm in their convictions, and both determined to remain unchanged.

He embraced her. "If you're so concerned about me, love me a little. That's what I need from you, not criticism."

I love you a lot, darling, she thought, *but you don't want my kind of love*.

She responded to his touch, and he drew back mollified. "That's better, but I'm still mad at you. I had intended to take you to the Black Hills tomorrow, but, since you've been snooping around, I've changed my mind."

"Oh, I've never been to the Black Hills," she said brightly. "I'll enjoy that."

"We're not going now. You should have thought of that before you criticized me."

They sat wrapped in each other's arms until long after nightfall, saying very little. The full moon cast dark shadows around them. Finally, Darren, seemingly over his pout, said, "Let's take a ride in the moonlight, Ginger. This is too good of an opportunity to miss."

They rode until long after midnight. Moonbeams turned the white cattle into phantoms, and the whole area seemed enchanted. They paused beside the lake and listened to the ripples lapping against the bank as waterfowl moved quietly in the rushes. When a brisk wind brought coolness to the night, they returned to the house.

He kissed her goodnight at her bedroom door and said, "I'll waken you about six o'clock. We want to get an early start for the Black Hills."

Chapter Seven

What a fascinating place! Ginger thought as she and Darren stood in a visitors' center and gazed at the South Dakota mountain where sculptor Gutzon Borglum had carved the faces of four American presidents—George Washington, Thomas Jefferson, Abraham Lincoln, and Theodore Roosevelt.

The day had been full and rewarding. They had toured Deadwood, where Wild Bill Hickock and Calamity Jane had made history. Darren had insisted upon taking a helicopter ride around the Mount Rushmore Monument, and they had seemed almost face-to-face with the colossal sculpture. They had driven through the Wind Cave National Park. But the day was almost over, and Ginger dreaded for it to end.

He could be such a wonderful companion, and Ginger wanted to forget his baser side. Yet, all day, off-and-on, she had remembered the impoverished children on the ranch. There were never any opportunities like this for them. If only there were some way that she could relieve the monotony of their lives.

While passing a shopping center on the outskirts of Rapid City, South Dakota, as they were returning to the ranch, Ginger asked, "Do you have time to stop here for a bit? There's something I want to buy."

He turned the truck in immediately. "Anything you want, sweetheart."

She got out of the truck and said, "I won't be long."

"I'll come with you. It's too hot to stay in the truck." She had hoped that he wouldn't, but he tagged along every step she took. She dawdled in the store, looking at inconsequential items, in the hope that he'd get disgusted with her and leave.

At last he said, "Ginger, if you want to shop, there are hundreds of stores in Lincoln better than this. We have a long way to drive, and I don't mind if you want to buy something, but you're just fooling around. This isn't like you."

With a blush, she said, "I want to buy a gift for Patrick."

He pointed to the rear of the store. "The toy department is back there. Come on."

She ignored him as she inspected the games and sports equipment. Finally, flushing under his gaze, she chose a pull-along toy for Patrick, then some coloring books, crayons, a doll, some building blocks, a set of horseshoes, and a ball and bat! She hesitated between a football and a basketball set, but she laid both of them aside. They cost more than she could afford.

Darren said lightly as they waited in line at the check-out counter, "Don't you think Patrick is a bit young for a set of horseshoes?" She didn't answer him, but Ginger knew that he had guessed her intentions when she took her billfold from her purse, and he put his hand over hers. "Ginger, I'll pay for this."

"No," she said determinedly, and he didn't argue. She had been saving money for a new evening coat to look nice for him when they went out next winter. But if he was going to be stingy with his employees, then he could just look at her old coat. She had a coat, and those kids didn't have any toys.

She excused herself to the ladies room, and Darren said, "Surely you'll allow me to carry your packages to the truck."

He made no more reference to the toys until they were almost home. About a mile from the ranch hands' houses he said, "Do you want to deliver your purchases now?"

She glanced sideways to see if he were making fun of her, but it wasn't ridicule that she saw in his eyes. "That will be fine," she answered. "Take them to Mildred's house. She can distribute them tomorrow."

Mildred's children tumbled out of the house at their approach, and little Ruth threw herself into Ginger's arms when she handed her the doll. The other items she left to Mildred's discretion. As Darren unloaded the games, Ginger noted that the basketball set and football were among them! He smiled broadly and winked at her when she saw him with the extra toys. He evidently had done a little shopping of his own while she had been in the restroom.

He drew her into the circle of his arm as they drove away, nibbled her ear, and said, "You're a pretty special person, Miss Prude."

"Thanks for buying the football and basketball," she said humbly. "They were too expensive for my budget, but I'll be happy to think of those boys playing with them."

"Ginger, I know you couldn't have much extra money. What were you planning to buy with the money you spent on those kids?"

"I was saving for a new winter coat, but my old one will do quite well."

"Doesn't it say in the Bible that, if you have two

coats, you're supposed to give one to someone who has none?"

Amazement must have shown on her face, because he arched his eyebrows, and said, "Don't look so surprised, Miss Prude. My parents were Christians, and they took me to church until I was old enough to know better." She didn't retort, because she knew that he was teasing her, but she looked at him suspiciously. "Don't you dare buy me a coat!" she said quickly.

He threw back his head and laughed loudly. "What makes you think I'd do a thing like that?"

"Because it's just like you. I can't mention a thing I don't have without you getting notions."

"I'd buy you a mink coat if you'd have it."

She drew away from him. "Now, don't you dare. I won't wear it."

"I know that, so I'll refrain. I don't have room in my safety deposit box to store a mink coat like I had to do that diamond and emerald necklace you refused."

"You mean you didn't return that necklace?" she demanded incredulously.

"Of course, I didn't return it. I bought that for you, and I intend to keep it until you come to your senses and start wearing it." He pulled her close to him again. "Now come over here and stop wasting time. We just have one more day left, you know."

When they drove into the garage, Darren turned off the ignition and kissed her long and passionately, kindling the familiar sensations which he aroused in her constantly now. She stirred in his embrace, and pillowed her head on his shoulder. "Only one more day," she whispered regretfully.

"You don't have to leave. Let's stay another week."

"But my job?"

He laughed as he nibbled softly on the fingers she'd

lifted to his face. "I'm the boss there, sweetheart. Do you think anyone would dare say anything if I told them you were taking another week?"

"Not to you, but *I'd* hear enough about it." She sighed. "I'll have to leave, but I don't want to. Maybe this is a good time to tell you that this has been the most wonderful week of my life. I don't suppose I'll ever be as happy again."

"You funny kid, you can come back anytime you want to."

"Oh, you'll bring someone else the next time."

He held her at arm's length. "Why, Ginger, I haven't brought *any* other woman up here!"

"My room has been used."

"So what? I've slept in there myself. Plus, I occasionally entertain business associates, and a few have brought their wives. But I've never been here alone with any woman before. I come home to relax, not to have someone troubling me."

"Then I haven't been any trouble to you?"

He kissed her long and ardently. "You've caused me plenty of trouble, but not the kind you mean."

"I have to go back anyway."

"If I had my way," he said, "I'd keep you up here all the time, to come home to." How Ginger wished the same thing, but she knew that would cost him a price he was unwilling to pay.

"I knew we'd be late, so I told Melissa not to bother cooking for us. I'm going to prepare our supper tonight."

"You?" Ginger asked in surprise.

"I have one talent as a cook. I can grill steaks and bake potatoes, so we're going to have steaks on the patio. While I broil those, you're going to make some salad. And Melissa probably left some dessert around someplace."

Darren changed into a pair of denim shorts and a red shirt, and soon had steaks sizzling on the patio grill. Ginger could smell the aroma of the meat as she made a salad. *Why does the week have to end?* she wondered. *If we could just stay here and shut out the rest of the world, he'd be a perfect mate.*

The ringing of the phone signaled that the world was intruding. Darren called from the patio, "Be a good girl and answer the phone. I can't leave the steaks. If it's Ike, I'll return his call."

Maureen Rowley, not Ike, was telephoning. For a moment, she didn't answer Ginger's "hello"; then she asked, "Melissa?"

Ginger remained silent, for she didn't want anyone at the Midland Bank to know where she'd spent her vacation. But Maureen finally said, "Is this Ginger?"

"Yes," Ginger answered hesitantly.

Maureen gave a nasty laugh. "Well, well, well," she said. "I suppose Mr. Banning is there, too. I thought it was strange that he didn't give me any instructions about where to contact him."

Ginger didn't answer.

"I hate to interrupt your little lovenest," Maureen said sarcastically, "but I have an important message for Mr. Banning."

Her face must have mirrored her distress, for, when she appeared on the patio, Darren asked quickly, "What is it?"

"Maureen wants to talk to you."

Darren looked annoyed, but he went inside to the phone, and Ginger returned to her salad-making. The conversation was short. Darren listened to what Maureen had to say, and answered. "I'll be in the office on

127

Monday morning. You can set up an appointment for him at one o'clock," and hung up the receiver.

Ginger looked at him in dismay. "Now everyone will know I'm up here!"

"What difference does it make?" he said. "We haven't done anything to be ashamed of." He dropped a quick kiss on her lips before he went back to the grill, but Ginger knew that very few people would believe that.

They ate their meal at twilight, and later sat together on the deck, watching the moon rise over the lake. They didn't talk all the time, finding that it was enough just to be together. Darren finally stirred and said, "I have some book work to do tonight. If you'll entertain yourself, I'll finish my records, and tomorrow we'll do what you want to."

"I'll load the dishwasher," Ginger said, "to save Melissa the trouble. Will it be all right if I stay downstairs with you?"

He kissed her. "Certainly, if you won't talk to me. I like having you near, Miss Prude."

Ginger laid aside her knitting. Patrick's sweater was finished, and she didn't want to start anything else. She glanced toward Darren's office, but the adding machine was still clicking, indicating that he hadn't finished his work. She wandered over to the bookshelves to find something to occupy her until he was free. Surprised to see a Bible, she decided to read her nightly chapters now.

The name, "Mary Banning," was printed in the fading gold on the front of the well-read Bible. *His mother*, she supposed. After reading a while, she turned through the Bible, until she came to the family records. Surely he wouldn't mind if she read about his antecendents. Johnny and Mary Banning had only one child, Darren, born November 27, thirty-five years ago.

Ginger's eyes bulged, her heart beat rapidly, and a cold chill flashed over her as she read the next entry. Darren Banning, married to Rhonda Eisel, sixteen years ago! Rhonda Banning's death was recorded a year later, and, on the same day, a *son* had been born!

"Oh, my goodness," she gasped. "Why did I have to find this?"

Distressed over her newfound knowledge, Ginger hadn't noticed that activity had ceased in the office. She had no inkling that Darren was near—until she looked over her shoulder, and he was watching her.

She felt her face burning. "Darren, I didn't mean to snoop. I was just reading the Bible while I waited for you, and I came to this. Don't be angry."

He didn't seem to be angry. "I should have told you before," he said glumly. He reached for the Bible, closed it, and put it back on the shelf. "Just forget you've seen it."

He turned on the television, and came to sit beside her. They sat silently, hand-in-hand, through a whole hour of television. Ginger had no idea what the program was about, and she doubted that Darren did either. Emotional undercurrents jarred the room's normal serenity.

"Bedtime," Darren said at last. "Do you want me to take you to your room?"

"No." She scampered off the couch, eager to be alone to think.

"My work is finished now," he said, "and I can spend tomorrow with you."

Ginger hurried to her bedroom. She hadn't supposed it was possible to be jealous of a dead woman, but she resented the fact that Rhonda Banning once had shared Darren's life. Had he possessed such a great love for her that he couldn't love anyone else?

Ginger lay awake for a long time. *Why won't he talk about his past? What about the son? Did he die, too? If not, he would be fifteen years old now.* She remembered the way Darren had acted when she'd asked him once if he'd wanted a son. What had happened in his few months of marriage to make him determined never to marry again?

She was still awake when a soft knock sounded on the door. "Ginger, are you awake?"

"Yes."

"May I come in for a minute?"

"Yes," she answered hesitantly. She sat up when he entered the room and pulled the covers tightly about her. He sat on the bed several minutes before he said anything.

"I told you to choose what we'd do tomorrow, but do you mind if *I* make the decision? I want to take you to Colorado."

"No, I don't mind," she said tenderly. "I'll go wherever you want."

He made no move to touch her. "We'll get up early then. I'll awaken you."

They arrived at the Denver airport by mid-morning. Darren rented a car for them and drove southeast along Highway 40. He hadn't given Ginger any indication of their destination, and she hadn't asked him. She dreaded the day's outcome, and wanted to delay the trauma as long as possible.

"I've been well-traveled since I've taken up with you," she said lightly, hoping to tease him out of his somber mood. "I had never been in South Dakota and

130

Colorado before this week."

He reached for her hand. "I'll take you any place you want to go, Miss Prude. Just name it—no strings attached."

She wanted to say, "I'd like to go see my mother," but she knew better. It wouldn't take him long to present her with a plane ticket to Saudi Arabia.

After driving for about an hour, Darren stopped before a small farmstead. The residence was a one-story house, probably containing four rooms. A few feet behind the house was a small structure and a few orderly outbuildings.

"This is my birthplace, Ginger. My parents lived here all of their lives." She looked at him in wonder, as he continued, "When Rhonda and I were married, we lived in *that* little house."

She patted him on the shoulder. "You have come a long way, haven't you?" she marveled, comparing his present financial status to this humble beginning. Obviously Darren had not inherited any money, but had made it all himself.

"I know you think I'm unappreciative of what you've made of yourself," she said, "but I don't mean it that way. I have a great deal of respect for your intellect and your dauntless energy. You're the most wonderful person I've ever known, and I do value your friendship. I only wish that your values were different, and that you put your energy to more humane pursuits."

"I understand that, Ginger," he said surprisingly. "And I'd like to become the kind of person you want me to be. But I've been this way too long. I'm set in my ways."

"Do you still own this place?" she asked, changing the subject.

"Yes, but I rent it, rather than operate it myself. There isn't any money in it. I just keep it for sentimental reasons."

"Is this what you brought me to see?" she asked.

"Partly, I guess," he said as he continued along the highway. Passing a small church and cemetery, he pointed. "That's where my parents went to church. They're buried there. Rhonda, too."

After the way he had acted last night, Ginger didn't suppose that he would comment on his marriage again, but he seemed to have no inhibitions about it. The knowledge was still too new and disturbing to her, however, and she couldn't ask any questions.

Darren drove for another fifty miles, and then stopped beside a brick building situated among a grove of spruce trees. The sign at the entrance read, "Mountain View Children's Home." Ginger was beginning to suspect what she'd find here—and she dreaded the knowledge.

Darren didn't get out of the car at first; he just sat staring at the building. Finally, with an effort, he said, "Come on, Ginger."

Inside the lobby of the institution, she waited while he made inquiries at the receptionist's desk. Darren's face was pale as he led her down a hallway. His pressure on her hand numbed her fingers, but, when she wiggled them, he eased his grasp. They passed several closed doors, and an atrium filled with greenery, chairs, and couches.

Ginger's heart was pounding so fast that she could hardly breathe. When Darren stopped before the last room in the hallway, she wondered if this had been the way Pandora had felt before she had opened the box. What was behind this door to upset Darren in this way? How would this new knowledge affect her love for him?

He drew a deep breath, opened the door, and motioned for her to go in. The room's occupant was restrained in a wheelchair. "Ginger," Darren said bitterly, "meet Darren Banning, Jr."

The emaciated body of a boy was slumped in the wheelchair, his head drawn sideways. His broad face, slanted eyes, slack facial muscles, large tongue, and protruding lower lip were obvious characteristics of Down's syndrome. The boy uttered unintelligible sounds.

Ginger was aware that Darren was watching her, not the boy, and she threw her arms around him, crying in pity, "Oh, my dear, my dear." She had never seen such sadness and hopelessness in anyone's eyes before. Darren crushed her to him in an embrace that almost stopped her breath. His body was trembling, and he whispered, "I can't stand it, Ginger."

The boy was still gibbering at them. "Let's go out for a minute, Darren," she said. "We can come back later." She led him down the hall to the atrium, which was blessedly empty. Sitting with him on the couch, she kept her arms around him until he gained control of his emotions.

Now she understood many things which had puzzled her—his cold reaction to her work with the handicapped, why he had ignored her remark about having a son, and the reason that he devoted all of his energies to accumulating a fortune.

"Now, tell me about it, darling," she said.

He began to talk with an effort, but soon the words flowed freely, as if he were eager to rid himself of the haunting past. "You saw in the Bible last night I'd been married. Rhonda and I met during our last year in high

133

school. We had a whirlwind courtship and then got married. I suppose we were as happy as two kids could be, who were saddled with a pregnancy right away, and had just a little money. I don't know what went wrong, but when the baby was born, Rhonda died.

"Mother took the boy, and, although the doctors warned us that he had brain damage, we wouldn't believe it. I was building all my future hopes in him."

Something occurred to Ginger. "The pony at the ranch is his."

Darren nodded. "Yes, I bought it on his first birthday before I finally accepted his condition. When Mother died, I didn't have the courage to sell Blacky. A foolish thing to do, I suppose, for, everytime I see the pony, I'm reminded of this," he motioned down the hall, "and my own inadequacy."

"We took the child to countless doctors," he continued, "but they couldn't do anything. We brought him here when the doctors convinced us it was the kindest thing we could do. Mother was physically exhausted with his care. I haven't been here since my mother died two years ago. I used to come with her, but I've lacked the courage to come alone. But I can't forget. If nothing else, I'm reminded every month when I send a check for his room and board."

Ginger kissed him on the forehead, and he hugged her gratefully. "I don't know that there's any reason for you to have to come if it upsets you so much. He doesn't know you, does he?"

"He's never known anything. It's been terrible, Ginger, never to hear him talk. He hasn't walked. Nothing. But I do feel some responsibility to know how they're caring for him."

"I want to go back in, Darren. You don't have to come."

He followed her down the hall and watched from the doorway as she went to the boy. Kneeling beside him, Ginger talked to him kindly. The gibbering continued, and she detected no sign of comprehension on his face.

"Let's take him outside for a minute," she said. Darren walked beside her as she wheeled the chair along the paved walks segmenting the broad lawn. They saw other patients, some not as retarded as Darren, Jr., but many others whose families were doubtlessly as torn emotionally as Darren was.

Taking leave of the boy back in his room, Darren placed a hand on his son's shoulder, and said, "Goodbye, son."

When they reached the automobile, Darren slumped over the steering wheel and sobbed. Comprehending the depth of his despair, Ginger wanted to help him. Lacking the insight to know what to say, she simply locked her arms tightly around his waist, leaned her head on his back, and cried with him. Her tears soaked the back of his coat, but, the way that he gripped the hands that she clenched around him, Ginger didn't think that he minded.

Emotionally spent, he leaned back. "Will I ever get over it, Ginger? Will I ever be able to come here without having it tear me up like this?"

While he had cried, Ginger had thought about the real reason why he was upset over his son. She had noted the words, "my own inadequacy." Was he so strong and virile that he couldn't reconcile the idea that his son wasn't perfect? Everything he touched turned out well; why not his son? She sensed that his mania for wealth and power came from the desire to prove to the world and himself that he was superior.

Praying for wisdom to answer him, she said, "You won't, until you stop blaming yourself."

"Whom else can I blame? You probably understand that this is the reason I never intend to marry again. I won't take a chance on producing another child like that!" He stirred in the seat and said, "We have to start home. Be a good girl and drive back to the airport for me. This car handles about like yours."

He walked around to her side of the car, and she slid under the steering wheel. "I can't pilot the plane, you know," she said smilingly.

"I'll be all right by then. Today has just unnerved me. That was the first time I'd touched the boy since we put him in here twelve years ago."

She tried to reason with him as they drove northward. "Darren, you're foolish to blame yourself for the child's condition. I've studied about the handicapped, and there could be dozens of reasons why your son didn't develop properly. It could have resulted from drugs your wife was taking. Wasn't it about that time that some drugs were causing multiple births, and children without limbs? Maybe that's what caused his disability. And the chances are minimal that you'd ever have another retarded child."

"But there *is* a chance, isn't there?"

"I suppose so."

"That's what I know, and I never intend to take that risk," he said with determination. "If it cost me my fortune, I'd *never* suffer again what I've lived through the past fifteen years." The finality in his voice quenched any hopes that Ginger had entertained about their future.

Melissa had long since retired when they returned to

the ranch. They had not eaten dinner, but they found a meal waiting for them on the kitchen table. Afterward, they sat beside the pool, the moonlight bright about them, and the dribbling fountain flowing softly in the quiet night.

"No one in Nebraska knows about my son," Darren said, and Ginger kissed the hand she was holding. His secret was safe with her.

Darren had the plane in position for take-off, but he hesitated, the engine idling.

"Is something wrong?" Ginger asked.

His face was bleak this morning, and Ginger's heart ached because of the frustration that he was experiencing. He had ceased hiding his sadness from her, although she was sure that he would continue presenting a self-satisfied front to the rest of the world.

"I don't want to go back, Ginger. I wish we could stay here forever and shut out the rest of the world," he said, echoing her thoughts. He smiled slightly. "You're the best thing that's ever happened to me, Miss Prude. I'll never be able to repay you for the way you stood by me yesterday."

"You don't have to repay me." She wanted to add, "I love you, Darren," but, even yet, she didn't quite dare.

"We've had such a good week, and I dread returning to Lincoln. When the everyday world comes crowding in on me, I'll be cantankerous with you like I've always been."

"Maybe things will be different after this."

"I doubt it." He unbuckled his seat belt and leaned toward her. His mouth nibbled at her throat before he brushed her lips with eager kisses that left her weak and panting. That engulfing warmth spread through her body, and she recognized the emotion that she

137

was beginning to crave as well as to dread. She gloried in his mastery over her emotions, and whispered, "Darren, I...," but her mind took control of her heart, and she gently eased away from him, without telling him of her love—the most precious gift she had to offer.

Darren Banning drew a deep breath, piloted the Beechcraft into the air, circled the ranch, and headed toward Lincoln.

Chapter Eight

Maureen had lost no time in broadcasting the news of Ginger's week at Darren's ranch. Upon her return to the bank, Ginger couldn't determine whether her fellow workers looked at her with more or less respect, but she sensed a difference in their attitude toward her. Throughout the week, no criticism of Darren was voiced in her presence.

Tina hadn't changed though. "I see he hasn't broken your heart yet," she said. "Maybe I was wrong about him."

"You *are* wrong about him," Ginger assured her.

"The bets are flying as to how long you'll last," Tina said. "Confidentially, I'm betting on you. I don't think he'll get rid of you as quickly as he has the others. So my money's on you, kid. And I'm overjoyed to see Maureen taken down a notch or two! Frankly, I can't stand the woman."

Darren was busy and hardly noticed Ginger's existence on Monday, but, on Tuesday afternoon, her phone rang just as she was leaving the bank. "Tonight?" Darren asked. They agreed to drive to Omaha for dinner.

Every night after that they were together, playing

139

the week away, knowing their subsequent meetings would be hampered when Ginger's classes started the next week .

"Ginger, I wish you wouldn't go to school this winter," he said when he kissed her good-bye on Saturday night.

"It isn't fair for you to expect that of me. You average being in Lincoln a week out of every month. What am I supposed to do the rest of the time—twiddle my thumbs and wait for you? Besides, I want to feel that I've accomplished something in life. I have a future to think about, you know."

"I know I'm selfish," he agreed, "but it's frustrating to have maybe only one night in town, and have you spend the whole time in class with Ken."

"You should be grateful that Ken goes with me. Would you want me walking around alone on the campus at night?"

"No," he admitted grudgingly. "But that's beside the point. You see more of him than you see of me, and I don't like it."

She might have pointed out that there was one way he could see more of her, but she still hadn't decided if she would marry him, even if he asked her. Now that she knew about his previous marriage, and his worries about his progeny, she could understand his hesitancy to take another wife. She wasn't sure that she could be happy as his wife, either. With his absolute refusal to believe that he needed any help in managing his life, he would never turn to God. Ginger doubted that she could have a happy life with a godless husband.

Ginger was beginning to believe that her and Darren's friendship was leveling off to a less frustrating affair when trouble erupted again over Mrs. Gainer's stock.

One afternoon, Tina pointed out a stately-looking gentleman going into Darren's office. "That's my grandfather," she said proudly. "He's decided to sell his stock to the Big Boss."

Ginger didn't think that Darren would want to bother with a stock transfer today, because he was leaving for California. He had hinted none too subtly that she accompany him, and, when she had ignored his hint, he had been petulant about it. At least he didn't seem to have any notion of taking Maureen.

Ginger supposed that Darren would be happy to get the stock certificates, but he didn't seem pleased when he crossed the lobby with Stuart Alleman to arrange their business transaction. His face mirrored his anger, and she wondered what had happened to displease him. She didn't find out, for, as soon as the transaction was over, Darren left immediately. Lincoln would be a lonely town now; when Darren came back from California, he was going to the ranch for the fall round-up. She wouldn't see him for several weeks!

"Have you heard the latest?" Tina asked.

Never knowing what Tina might be discussing, Ginger simply shook her head.

"I didn't tell you, because, with you being so close to the Big Boss, I figured you already knew. But then I decided, since he'd been in California, you may not have seen him since it happened."

"Since *what* happened?" Ginger asked.

"Grandfather made the Big Boss pay through the nose for those stock certificates," Tina continued. "You see, there's *another* stockholder who's trying to buy extra stock. That man had offered $150.00 per share, and Grandfather was going to sell to the other man if Banning didn't buy!

"I guess he hit the ceiling, threatened, swore, and everything else imaginable, but Grandfather held fast. Mr. Banning either had to buy the stock that day, or lose his chance."

No wonder he was angry, Ginger thought, *but why has he been avoiding me*? He'd been back from California for several days now and he hadn't looked at her. Not even a hello.

Tina was still chatting, and Ginger picked up the theme of her talk. "Someone told Mrs. Gainer how much he'd paid for this latest stock, and she's *suing him* for the additional amount she thinks is due her. He's been summoned to a court hearing next week."

And he thinks I told Mrs. Gainer! Ginger thought.

All afternoon, she pondered whether she should say anything to him. When her balancing was done for the day, she crossed the lobby to his office.

"Mr. Banning isn't seeing anyone," Maureen told her coldly.

Maureen's haughty manner didn't daunt Ginger anymore. She knew Darren cared nothing for the woman. "Is there anyone in the office with him?"

"No."

"Then he'll see me," Ginger said and walked to the inner office door.

"It must be wonderful to feel so sure of yourself," Maureen said sarcastically as Ginger opened the door.

He was sitting at the desk, but he wasn't working. He was just staring into space. He turned to face Ginger, and his eyes were unfriendly.

She leaned over the desk. "I didn't tell Mrs. Gainer," she said.

He didn't respond for a bit, but searched her face to

discern the truth. "Somebody did."

"You must trust me a lot," she said gravely. "Do you actually think I'd double-cross you that way?"

"But you've said all along that I should have paid her more!"

He was softening a little, and she smiled at him. "I still think you should, but you underestimate me, Darren, if you think I'd ever discuss that with anyone else. I might criticize you to your face, but no one else has ever heard me say anything against you."

"Then who did tell her?" he asked.

"I don't know, but I'll find out tonight. I didn't even know what you paid for the Alleman stock until Tina told me today."

"Maybe Tina told the Gainer woman," he postulated.

"I doubt it, but it doesn't matter, as long as you know I didn't."

"It matters a dickens of a lot to me," he retorted. "Anytime you get mixed up with lawyers, it costs! And besides the money it may cost me, I need to get up to the ranch, and now this court hearing is delaying me. Anyway, Miss Prude, I'm glad it wasn't you." He stood up and held out his hand to her. "Come here."

He drew her around the desk into the circle of his arms. "Two weeks is too long not to kiss you. You should have gone to California with me."

"What if someone comes in?" Ginger protested. "Can't we wait until tonight for this?"

"No! I would have an appointment on the only night you're free."

"You shouldn't be such an important man, and you'd have lots of free time."

"Stop talking, and kiss me," he ordered. Ginger had missed him, and time and place were forgotten as she

143

returned his caresses without hesitation. When he drew away, his eyes were glowing and the worried look was gone from his face. She *was* good for him and she knew that.

"Thanks for coming in, Ginger. It was tearing me up inside to think you'd double-crossed me. I can stand anything but having you against me. I'd lose a million dollars before I'd lose you."

His eyes almost worshiped her. *Why can't he see we can't go on this way indefinitely? I can't stand to lose him either, but it's frustrating to never be sure of him. Just a day at a time,* she thought, as she often had before.

The outer door opened, and Maureen barged in. Darren tightened his embrace and kept Ginger in his arms. Ginger detected resignation on Maureen's face, as if the secretary realized at last that there was no hope for her. "Are you available to answer your phone?" she asked. Neither of them had been aware of the buzzing of his telephone.

"No, I'm busy. Take the number, and I'll return the call." He gathered Ginger close again and chuckled softly in her ear. "Don't look so guilty, sweetheart. Everyone knows anyway. And, since they do know, you might as well wear the gift I brought you from California." He took a box from his desk and held it open for her to see. The gift was a golden brooch, with three large diamonds forming a triangle, and a lustrous "G" monogrammed between the diamonds.

He finally had worn down her resistance, and she didn't protest as he removed the costume jewelry from the front of her blouse. Replacing it with his gift, it was as if he had proclaimed to the world that he'd put his brand on her as he had his other possessions.

144

"Mrs. Gainer!" Ginger accosted her neighbor as soon as she arrived home. "I want to know who told you the price of the Alleman stock."

"I really don't know. *Someone* telephoned me one day, and said, 'Here's a little tip that might interest you. Darren Banning just paid $150.00 per share for Stuart Alleman's bank stock.' Maybe it's wrong for me to sue him, but the difference in what he paid Alleman, and what he wants to pay me, amounts to $25,000.00. That would make a big difference in my security. Don't you think I'm right?"

Ginger did think that she was right, but she wasn't going to admit it. "Was the caller a man or a woman?"

"Oh, it was a woman!"

"But you know it wasn't me, don't you? Mr. Banning thought I had told you."

"Oh, no, it wasn't you," Mrs. Gainer said without hesitation. "I'd have recognized your voice."

"Then please tell Mr. Banning that."

"I'm afraid to speak to the man," Mrs. Gainer said. "You can't imagine how he talked to me when he received notice of my lawsuit. I finally hung up on him."

They were no nearer to an answer than before. Tina might have phoned Mrs. Gainer, so Ginger was careful of what she said to her friend.

Ginger and Darren were together only one night that week, and he was so irritable that Ginger found it hard to cope with him. He was particularly grumpy when she avoided his advances.

The bank personnel were wary of him, and the day the lawyers and clients met for a preliminary hearing, all the employees dreaded the outcome. The minute that he returned to the bank, Ginger knew from the wicked gleam in his eye that he had won.

Approaching Maureen's desk, Darren said, "Get the Gainer certificates ready for transfer at my original contract. Even her lawyer had to admit that they had no grounds for a lawsuit! They'll be here soon for the final transaction."

Ginger was depressed when Mrs. Gainer and her lawyer came in later on in the day. Ginger's neighbor looked as if the spirit had been stamped out of her, but she waved to Ginger, who tried to give her an encouraging smile. She knew that the loss of the money was a big blow to the older woman, and Darren wouldn't have missed it.

As Mrs. Gainer passed Maureen's desk on her exit from the bank, the phone rang, and Maureen answered it. "Good afternoon, Mr. Banning's office," she said in her usual manner.

Mrs. Gainer stopped suddenly, and turned to Darren, who still was standing in the doorway of his office. The widow exclaimed, "Why, that's the woman who told me what you'd paid for the Alleman stock, Mr. Banning. I recognize her voice."

Maureen grimaced. Ginger never had seen Darren more furious, but he waited until Mrs. Gainer and her lawyer had left before he let the hatchet fall. "Get out!" he shouted. "Clean out your desk and take your disloyal face out of my sight! If you aren't out of this building in an hour, I'll brand you all over the state for the double-crosser you are."

He slammed the door as he returned to his office, and Maureen sat as if she'd turned to stone.

"Why would Maureen take a chance of making him mad?" Ginger whispered to Tina. "What's Mrs. Gainer to her?"

"I doubt she even knew the Gainer woman. She probably thought the Big Boss would blame you for telling his business, and, if Banning was mad at you, he might take up with her again. Who knows?"

In a short time, Maureen's office was empty. Ginger almost wished she had stayed, for she knew that Darren cared nothing for her. How could she stand it, if he moved another siren into the room across the lobby?

Ginger munched on a peanut butter and pickle sandwich while she did some last-minute studying for her child psychology course. When the phone rang, she was tempted not to answer it, fearing that Mrs. Gainer was calling to berate Darren.

"Ginger, will you cut your class and have dinner with me?" Darren pleaded when she answered.

Oh, my dear, she thought, *why can't you understand that I have some other responsibility besides to you?* She replied, "There's a test tonight. I can't miss it."

"But I need to talk to you," he said.

"We had dinner together last night. We talked then."

"I'm leaving in the morning. Please, Ginger!" he begged, something which was so out-of-character for him that she relented.

"If I go and take the test during the first half of the session, you could meet me at the university at about eight o'clock. Sometimes the professor dismisses us after a test anyway. If not, Ken can take notes for me. Will that be all right?"

"I suppose so," he said grudgingly. "And dress up, too. We're going to dine in style tonight."

He hadn't seen her latest creation, so Ginger put it on. She had made the dress of winter-white velour. Long push-up sleeves, a surplice front, and wide sashed belt gave the softly draped dress an elegant look. Her only jewelry was the diamond pendant that she'd accepted from him months ago.

A table for two in a quiet alcove, dim lights, and romantic violin music. Thinking of the traditional movies she'd seen, Ginger thought that this was a perfect setting for a marriage proposal!

But it wasn't marriage that Darren had in mind. As soon as their order was taken, he came to the point immediately. He took her hand and held it tightly. "Ginger, I want *you* to become my secretary now." She looked at him blankly as he talked persuasively. "Don't you see? This will be the perfect set-up. I won't have to be separated from you at all. You'd have every reason to be with me wherever I go."

She still stared at him, and he shifted a bit uncomfortably under her gaze. Her thoughts were busy, even if she was silent. *But what about my plans?* she thought. *Am I supposed to drop everything and run to you when you want me?* She was tempted, however. It would be one way to keep him from hiring another secretary to worry her. And she thought of all the exciting things they'd done together in the past few months. What would the future hold if she could go everywhere with him?

"Let me think!" she said. "Don't keep pressuring me."

Ginger contemplated while she consumed a cup of split pea soup, and a dinner which included filet mignon, steamed rice with snipped parsley, broccoli with cheese sauce, dilly bread, and perfection salad.

All the places she wanted to see passed through her mind—Big Ben, Saint Paul's Cathedral, Westminster Abbey in London, England; the Louvre, Versailles, Fontainebleau, Nice in France; Venice, Rome, Florence in Italy; The Parthenon and the Acropolis in Greece; and the Holy Land.

But Ginger's past training took over her thoughts, and she remembered the time when Jesus, too, had gone through His days of temptation. The Devil had reviewed all the kingdoms of the world and the glory of them, and had promised Jesus, "They'll be yours, if you'll fall down and worship me."

Ginger also thought of the episode at the swimming pool when she and Darren had been alone at the ranch. She couldn't always keep him at bay, especially when her own body cried out for him. If she did anything, she should *lessen* her association with him, not put herself in a position to be with him *constantly*, and in situations where she might not have the will to resist him.

She sensed the degradation that she would feel if she ever allowed him to use her body, and it was useless to hope that he'd want to marry her someday. Marriage wasn't in his plans for her, that was obvious.

As Ginger's eyes searched Darren's face, the Tempter said, "You'll lose him." *But if you lose your own self-respect, what will you have? And if he leaves you eventually, what would you have then? Nothing but a soiled life to offer someone else.*

Every time she looked up, Darren smiled invitingly at her. Tonight he was dressed in garments she hadn't seen before—a luxurious two-button onyx blazer with goldtone/black enamel buttons, and silk blend slacks of silver gray. His dress shirt, of a rich claret shade with white admiral collar and cuffs, blended with the white dotted tie. A white silk handkerchief stood out vividly in his breast pocket against the coat's dark background.

Lord, give me the strength to resist this temptation,

she prayed silently. As Darren sat before her, so handsome, dear, and precious, she wondered if the Tempter had appeared to Jesus in such a magnificent form.

She declined dessert, and, after the waiter had left them, Ginger said, shaking her head slowly, "No, Darren, I won't take the job."

He must have accepted the finality in her voice, for he flushed angrily, and said, "Your prudish principles are rearing their nasty heads again."

He knew why she refused, so why bother to explain? She wanted to say, "I'd make you a better wife than a secretary," but she said instead, "For one thing, Darren, I'm not a secretary. I'm a mediocre typist, and I don't know shorthand, and it wouldn't be long until you'd see that you need someone to really handle your business, not keep you company. And you can scoff at my 'prudish' qualities if you want to, but you've known all along that I had them. If you were the kind of man you should be, you'd help me retain my principles, instead of always throwing temptation into my way."

He took her home without another word. He made no move to kiss her good-bye, nor did he get out of the car and walk with her to the door. Another day? She doubted it now.

Before she went to bed, Ginger read the biblical account of Jesus' temptation, taking particular note that angels had ministered to Him at the end of his traumatic experience. Never before had Ginger needed the help of her faith as she cried herself through another sleepless night.

Patrick was demanding a good deal of attention, and Ginger was progressing slowly with her pie baking. He continually threw his ball out of the playpen, and

150

shouted until she got it for him. She almost had the final crust ready for the pan when the doorbell rang.

"Come in," she called, "it's unlocked." Darren walked in, and she smiled at him, hoping the sheer joy that he'd returned to her didn't show in her face. She hadn't seen him for over two weeks.

"Hi. Make yourself at home. I'll have these pies in the oven in a few minutes. I promised to take them to the church. They're having a dinner for senior citizens tonight."

Darren removed his coat, and eyed Patrick with disgust. "I see you've added baby-sitting to your activities. What next?"

Ginger noted his difficult mood; he probably was still peeved over her refusal to be his secretary.

"Sally's mother is sick, and I volunteered to keep Patrick while she helped on the farm. I had to stay home to make these pies anyway."

He glanced morosely out the window. A brisk wind was blowing dust around the countryside; winter wasn't far away. He sat down in the rocking chair, as far away from Patrick as he could get. "Well, I was hoping you could spare enough of your precious time to spend the evening with me. I believe you're the only person in the state of Nebraska who takes pity on every stray dog. You have time for everyone but me," he said peevishly.

She chose to ignore his sarcasm, and laughed as she said, "Be fair, Darren. I didn't know you'd be here this afternoon. What did you expect?"

"For just once, I'd like to have you act like you'd missed me and were glad to see me—waiting for ME, instead of looking after everyone else!"

She might have said that waiting for him was a fruitless task, but she didn't. "You could have phoned me

151

that you were coming. And besides, the way you acted when you left the last time, I didn't know if you'd ever come back."

"I'll always come back to you, Ginger," he said with an odd expression on his face.

"But I don't have any guarantee of that," she said, almost in a whisper.

She put the pies in the oven, wiped her hands, and went to him. He drew her down on his lap and kissed her hungrily. He kissed her closed eyelids, her throat, and back to her lips again. She locked her arms around his neck and nestled against his shoulder.

"I've missed you, Miss Prude," he admitted.

"Uh huh! Me, too," she murmured.

They had forgotten Patrick. At that moment the toddler shouted, threw the rubber ball, and struck Darren on the forehead. "That kid irritates me!" he growled.

But he laughed when Ginger said, "He doesn't like to be ignored either." She rolled off his lap. "Just relax while I clean the kitchen, and change my clothes. Sally should be back by the time the pies are baked, and we can spend the evening together."

He stretched out on the couch, his feet dangling over the edge. He was longer than the sofa. "I am tired. I've been on horseback from morning to night the past ten days, and I'm bone weary. We moved the cattle in close to the ranch so we can feed them this winter."

"How's Melissa and everybody at the ranch?" Ginger inquired.

"She kept busy feeding Ike and me. And the ranch hands are all right too. I think every woman I saw was pregnant, so there will be a new crop of kids for you to play with next summer."

Ginger smiled to herself as she rinsed the dishes. *Is*

he suggesting that I'll be going to the ranch again? Has he actually fooled himself into thinking that we can go on like this year after year? she thought sadly.

"And you want me to build new houses for them," he continued. "The way they increase, I'd have to add another room every year."

At least her comments had brought him to some consciousness of his responsibility. She didn't comment, and he talked on about the fall roundup.

"It's the best herd of calves we've had for years. I should net several thousand dollars more this year than last." He scowled at her when she smiled. "I suppose you're giving God credit for that, too, instead of the hard work Ike and I've done all summer."

"I didn't say a word."

"You didn't have to. I can read your mind by now. I know what you're thinking."

Oh, no, you can't, my darling, she thought, *or I'd have lost you before this. How long will it last?* she pondered. *How much longer can I keep him coming back to me?*

"Where are we going tonight?" Ginger asked when she finished the dishes. "What kind of clothes should I wear?"

"We'll go anywhere you want to go, and wear the beige outfit you were wearing the day we had that trouble about the Gainer stock. I didn't get to enjoy it then."

By the time that she had finished dressing, Sally still hadn't returned. The pies were ready, so Ginger suggested, "If you'll watch Patrick, I'll take these pies down to the church now. Sally should be here by the time I get back, and the evening will be ours."

"Now, Ginger, I've changed a lot of my habits to suit you, but I'm *not* playing nursemaid to that kid!"

153

Ginger pulled on a tan windbreaker, and put the pies in a carrying case. She left the lid ajar because the pastries were still hot.

"Ginger, I mean it. Don't leave me here with him!"

She leaned over and kissed him lightly on the lips. "It won't hurt you to watch him for fifteen minutes. If he cries, just ignore him." Without giving him further opportunity to protest, she left. Patrick and Darren were eyeing each other warily as she closed the door.

She was gone longer than she had expected. When she returned to the trailer, her heart warmed at the scene before her. Apparently Patrick had been crying, for tears were evident on his cheeks. Darren was sitting in her arm chair with Patrick held securely in his arms—and both of them were asleep. Ginger bent and kissed Darren softly on the forehead. She had never loved him more.

They didn't awaken until Sally came for Patrick. Sally looked surprised when she saw Darren holding her son, and she quickly took her departure. Then a sleepy Darren held out his arms and said, "Come here, vixen," and Ginger took up the place that Patrick had vacated. "I don't know why I let you get away with ordering me around."

Ginger abandoned herself more freely to his affection than she normally did. *Oh, just once let him say he loves me*, she thought. Surely she couldn't love a man this much, a man who gave all evidence of desiring her, and yet who returned none of her love. She suddenly felt degraded to be so attached to a man who wouldn't voice his feelings for her.

She smoothed back the hair from his forehead, and, for the first time, noted a few gray hairs along his temple. Although she didn't mention them, he must have noted her attention, for he said, "I know they're there, and you've given me most of those gray hairs, Miss Prude."

"Good. I'm glad I'm responsible. I like them. You'll look very distinguished with gray hair."

"Don't make an old man out of me yet," he grumbled. He settled back in the chair, and breathed deeply. "It's peaceful here."

Ginger's fingers traced the outline of his face, his eyebrows, his lips. "Would you like for me to prepare something to eat and us stay here? It was raining when I came in, and it won't be a good evening to be out."

"Sure, I'd like it. I'm always going someplace. It would be good just to stay home for a change."

Ginger kissed him affectionately on the nose. "All right, you stay right here. I made sauce this morning, and I'll cook some spaghetti in a few minutes. And I cheated on the senior citizens and kept one of their pies for you."

After their meal, he stretched out on the couch and went to sleep again. When she finished washing the dishes, she didn't awaken him because she knew that he was very tired. She sat nearby and took up her knitting.

He'd been watching her for a while before she realized he was awake. "What are you making now?" he asked. "Something for a vagrant, I suppose." She didn't answer, but, if he could have seen the *golden triangle* she'd embroidered on the sweater's pocket, he would have known to whom the garment would belong. Hardly a vagrant!

"Mildred Pederman said to tell you she was taking the kids to school now," Darren announced.

Her eyes widened. "How's she taking them?"

"In my van," he said shortly.

"What does she do while the children are in school?"

"She has a job as the school's cook," he said reluctantly.

"Did you get her the job?" she asked, her eyes shining.

"Yes," he answered gruffly.

Laughingly, she said, "Why are you so hesitant to admit that you helped them?"

He didn't answer, nor would he look at her as she laid aside her knitting and went to him. Sitting beside him on the couch, her eyes bright with pride, she said, "Did anyone ever tell you what a wonderful person you are, Mr. Banning?"

"No, but it wouldn't hurt for me to hear it occasionally," he grumbled.

"Let me tell you this way," she murmured as she bent over him. For the first time, she took the initiative in their intimacy. Her caresses plunged them to an ecstasy they'd never experienced before. This time it was Darren who put her off before the danger point was reached.

"You're a mystery to me, Miss Prude. I spend hundreds of dollars for things you won't use, and for which you barely thank me, but I do a favor for a bunch of worthless kids, and you show your gratitude in a way that reduces my defenses to nothing. Right now, if you asked me to give away my fortune, I'd probably do it."

Her fingers roamed playfully over his face and neck. "When you do things for 'worthless' people, expecting nothing in return, I know you're becoming that big man I want you to be."

He shook his head. "It was a sorry day for me when I took up with a woman who had a conscience."

156

"You don't have any regrets, do you?" she asked.

He turned on his side and pulled her down beside him on the couch. His kiss left no doubt of the answer.

Chapter Nine

Darren stayed in Lincoln only a couple of days before he left for South America. In that time, however, he hired a new secretary.

Ginger was aware of many conferences, and she wondered what was underway. She didn't find out until Tina Alleman was called into Darren's office for an interview. When she returned to her window, Tina whispered in Ginger's ear, "You won't believe this!" Then, as an afterthought she added, "Or maybe you know?"

As usual, Ginger hadn't an idea of what she meant—and she had to wait until lunchtime to find out.

"Do you know who the Big Boss has hired for his secretary?" Tina blurted out as soon as they were alone.

Ginger shook her head and waited breathlessly, dreading to hear the answer.

Tina laughed. "Me! To think I'd get a promotion like that, and all this time I've been expecting to be fired because of his trouble with Grandfather."

Ginger threw her arms around Tina's ample frame. "Congratulations!" She was ecstatically happy that Tina would be Darren's closest employee. "You see, he isn't nearly as bad as you think he is," Ginger said.

"You mean he isn't nearly as bad as he used to be," Tina retorted, as she swallowed the last of her sandwich. "You've changed him, Ginger. I don't know what you see in the man, and he isn't nearly good enough for you, but, if you want him, I hope you get him."

"There isn't any chance of that," Ginger assured her sadly.

Darren called Ginger to his office for a few minutes before he left. "Just a fast kiss before I leave, sweetheart," he requested. She went eagerly to his arms and closed her eyes when his mouth claimed hers. "It's harder and harder to leave you, Ginger."

"Why are you going this time?" she asked, even though she rarely inquired into his business affairs.

"Some of my associates and I are investing in some oil land in Venezuela. I don't know how long I'll be gone."

"Are you flying yourself?"

"As far as Florida, then we'll all go by commercial lines." He bent and kissed her again. "What do you want from South America?"

Her fingers fondled his ears. "Just you. Be careful, Darren." Her gaze roamed his face, for she wanted a vivid picture of his features to last her. Why did he have to be such a wonderful person? Why couldn't she put him out of her mind? "I like your choice for secretary, Mr. Banning."

His smile was sparkling. "I thought you would, Miss Prude."

Ken Grady blew the horn, and Ginger picked up her umbrella and hurried out to the driveway. *My, but the air is colder than it was this morning*, she thought as she got into his car. They were going to Hastings, a hundred miles to the west, to an afternoon seminar. The weather forecast predicted snow, and she would have preferred to skip the meeting, but she and Ken had been assigned to write a critique of the speaker's address.

"You'll need a fur coat instead of that umbrella," Ken said, "if it keeps getting colder." The morning's rain already had turned to a cold mist.

Before Ken had turned the car, Darren's white Cadillac stopped beside them. "Oh, I didn't know he was back, Ken," she said. "Will you wait a minute?"

"I'll have to," he said dryly. "He has the roadway blocked."

She hurried into the car beside Darren, and, without a greeting, he said irritably, "Now where are you going?"

"To Hastings College for a seminar we've been assigned to attend."

"Hastings!" he said, as though it were the end of the earth. "Why in the devil would you go out *there* with a university *here*?"

"The teacher conducting the seminar is an authority on Special Education," she explained patiently. She opened the door and started to get out. "I have to leave, Darren, or we'll be late. Surely you'll be here tomorrow."

"But I wanted to be with you now. I rushed like mad to get here, and now you're going to run off and leave me."

It was useless to remind him that she hadn't any idea of his return. They'd been through that many times before.

"Why can't I take you?" he offered.

160

"But what will you do for the three hours that we're in session?"

"I'll sleep. I haven't had any rest for a week." He did look tired, and that probably accounted for his irritability.

"This isn't very fair to Ken."

"Well, I don't want him, but you can invite him to ride with us, if you want to."

Ken was wise enough to refuse, and he seemed not to mind that Ginger chose to go with Darren. "I don't know why you bother with me, Ken. This isn't a very nice thing to do to you. But he's been gone for two weeks, and I don't see him very often."

Ken waved away her excuses, and drove off without her. Ginger soon found out the reason for Darren's irritation.

"I wasted a lot of money and time on this fool trip," he said angrily. "I don't think we'll ever get our money out of that investment." Most of the way to Hastings, he grumbled about the things that had gone wrong.

Ginger tried to soothe him out of his depression. She sat close to him, with her hand on his shoulder. "Don't worry about it, dear. It won't hurt you to lose some money. Besides, you can always deduct a loss from your income tax. In the long run, it may not be very bad."

"I don't like to fail at anything, Ginger."

She laughed. "No one will make perfect decisions every time, even if they do have the Midas touch, and one bad investment won't make you a failure." She was massaging the back of his neck to ease the tension she felt there, and he moved his head wearily to the pressure.

"That feels good, Miss Prude."

She leaned over and kissed his hand lying on the

161

steering wheel. "Besides, you don't know that the investment is lost, do you?"

"No."

"Then forget about it, and tell me what South America is like."

"It was empty," he said, "without you. That's one thing that aggravated me so much—every time we were ready to come home, something else would happen to delay us. All I could think about was getting back to you." He gave her a sour look. "Ginger, there are times when I dislike you heartily, and resent the way you've captivated my thoughts."

The intermittent rain had turned to snow and the wind was strong by the time they arrived at Hastings College. Darren observed, "I don't trust this weather, Ginger. I've seen blizzards in the fall. You come back as soon as you can."

But the seminar wasn't over until six o'clock, and, with the cloudy conditions, it was almost dark by then. Polar blasts of air buffeted Ken and Ginger as they walked from the building, and icy snow stung their faces. At least an inch of the white stuff was on the ground, and the air was full of blowing snow.

Darren was listening to the car radio. "Ken, the weather forecast doesn't sound a bit good. They're predicting a half-foot of snow with blizzard-like winds."

Ken got in the car and sat with them for a few minutes to listen to the latest predictions. "Ginger," he said, "under the circumstances, I think I'll stay here in Hastings with my aunt, rather than drive back alone in this weather. I don't have snow tires yet. Both of you are welcome to stay, too."

"Thanks, Ken," Darren said, "but I've done some

telephoning while you two were inside, and there are several business deals that have come up while I've been gone. I need to get back, but Ginger can stay if she wants."

She shook her head. "No, I'm going with you. I'd be worried all night with you out in this storm alone."

"Let's get started then. Take care, Ken."

The wind was so strong that Ken had trouble getting the door of the Cadillac closed, but he stood and watched them as they drove away. Darren drove slowly until they had left the town behind, and, even then, he couldn't gain any speed on the icy roads.

"I'm not going back on the Interstate," he said, "We may be better off to travel Highway 6. The police might close the Interstate and leave us stranded."

Visibility was almost zero. As they crept along slowly for the next twenty miles, they passed numerous stalled or wrecked vehicles. Sometimes the wind buffeted the Cadillac as though it were a feather.

The strain was telling on Darren, and Ginger became frightened when she saw his agitation. "Are you afraid, Darren?" she whispered after he had swerved and narrowly missed an oncoming automobile.

"Yes, I am," he admitted gruffly. "There's ice under this snow, and, with the gusty wind, I don't have control of the car half the time. We must find shelter before we have a wreck, or get stopped in stalled traffic. It doesn't matter about me, but I don't want anything to happen to you."

"But where can we go?"

"The next exit we come to, I'm going to get off. We might find a motel, a restaurant, or some place to spend the night. I'd stop at a farmhouse, but, with so much snow, I can't even see one, and it would be folly to leave the car to start looking."

A semitrailer was moving slowly in front of them. When the driver put on his signal light, Darren followed him. The truck pulled to one side, and Darren got out to talk to the driver. Ginger watched Darren in the Cadillac's headlights. He wasn't dressed warmly enough for such weather. His business suit was thin, and he was shivering when he returned.

"He says there's a small motel down the road a few miles, and he's heading there. We'll follow him."

Ginger was wishing that she'd stayed with Ken's aunt; somehow, she dreaded the night. When the truck pulled into a parking lot, they could see the dim outline of a one-story motel. Darren stopped the Cadillac close to the lobby entrance, and took her hand. "Stay close to me, so we won't get separated. Hurry."

The electric lights went off just as they got inside the lobby, but a candle burned on the counter. In the eerie light, they saw a woman rise from a desk. Suddenly the room flooded with light again.

"This has been going on for the last hour," the proprietor said. "The wind is disrupting the electric service. It's bad for our heat too because we have electric heaters in the rooms."

"Do you have any vacancies?" Darren inquired.

"Only one room with a double bed."

Ginger looked quickly at Darren. He ignored her as he said, "We'll take it," filled out the card, and paid the fee.

How could he? she thought. She wasn't going to make a scene in front of this woman, but, if he thought that she would share a room with him, blizzard or no blizzard, he had another thought coming.

The motel had a narrow porch running the length of the place, and their room was in the middle of the twelve units. Darren hustled her down the walkway, while the wind blew their clothes and numbed their faces and hands. He hardly could get the door unlocked because of his cold hands, and, just as they stepped inside, the lights went off again.

He slammed the door against the power of the wind. As though that were a signal, the lights blinked back on. The room was small, with meager furnishings, and the double bed loomed like some evil thing to Ginger.

"I won't sleep in here with you, Darren," she declared.

"Ginger, be reasonable. We don't have any choice. I can't risk your life and mine by going back out on the road in this storm. Besides, this room is like an icebox; you'll be *glad* to share the bed with me before morning."

Her face flushed in spite of the cold room. "There must be some other way."

"I don't intend to sleep on the floor, and I dare say you wouldn't like it either. I'm going to move the car down here, and, when I get back, you be in bed. There's no need to be foolish."

She still hadn't decided what to do when she heard him stop the Cadillac in front of their door, but, when he tried to get in, the chain nightlatch was hooked!

"Ginger!" he thundered above the noise of the wind.

"You've got to listen to me, Darren. I'm not going to let you in until you agree to reason. And stop shouting; I don't want everyone to know what's going on here."

"You'd better get out of the way," he shouted. With one powerful lunge, he forced the chain from its hook and burst into the room. She retreated until the room's one chair was between them. For the first time, she was actually afraid of him, even though he seemed to be making an effort to remain calm.

"Ginger, I didn't plan this, you know that. We can't go on, there aren't any more rooms, and it's too cold for me to sleep in the car. What will it hurt if we sleep in the same bed? We've snuggled up together before, and nothing has happened."

"No," she said, with head bowed.

"Who is it you don't trust—yourself or me?" he asked cruelly.

"That isn't fair, Darren."

"Well, are you being fair to me? You know you aren't. It's true that I promised I wouldn't push our relationship further than you wanted it to go, but don't you suppose *I* know how you feel when I kiss you? You want me as much as I want you, and you've kept me dallying for six months. I'm tired of it!"

She faced him bravely. "I'll admit it, I do desire you, but I'll never accept you on your terms."

"So you *do* have a price tag! What is it—a wedding ring? You don't want the other jewelry I buy you, but I suppose you'd gladly take a wedding ring," he said nastily.

"Why, Darren," she said. "I wouldn't marry you."

His surprise couldn't have been greater. "What do you mean you wouldn't marry me? If I promised to marry you tomorrow, you mean you wouldn't spend the night with me?"

"I wouldn't spend the night with you, nor would I marry you. Darren, we aren't good for each other. And as long as you scoff at my Christian beliefs, and have no faith yourself, a marriage between us would be a farce. It would be just as big a sin to marry you as it would to go to bed with you here tonight."

The lights went off again. Standing in the darkness, with the fury of the storm raging outside, she found

166

the courage to tell him what she'd never told him before. "If you were a different kind of person, darling, and if you wanted me, I'd gladly take my place as your wife, because *I love you*, Darren, more than my own life. I haven't told you that, because I was afraid you'd leave me if you knew the extent of my love. But it doesn't matter now, for I've decided that *I'm* the one who has to leave."

The overhead light blinked on, and, although the room was still dim, she could see his face clearly.

"Darren, I hate to say this, and I don't even want to believe it because I love you so much, but you aren't right for me. If I keep on seeing you, loving you as I do, the day will come when I'll submit to you, and I'd feel stained the rest of my life."

He stared at her, his face expressionless. The silence between them was suffocating.

She continued, "I'm going to turn in my resignation at Midland on Monday. There isn't any use for us to torture ourselves any longer."

"Where will you go?" he asked bleakly.

She shrugged her shoulders. "Some place away from Lincoln where you can't find me. Some place where I won't expect to see you every minute, or long to hear your voice. Some place where I can forget you. I don't suppose I'll *ever* stop loving you, but, for my own sake, I'll try hard enough."

She started past him to the door, and he caught her arm.

"I'll sleep in the car," she said. "You can have the room; you paid for it."

"You'll do nothing of the kind." He handed her the key. "You've won again, Miss Prude," he said without anger. "Lock yourself in. I'll sit in the lobby tonight. I hope you enjoy your icy bed."

The lights went off then for good, and, since Ginger didn't even have a flashlight, she groped for the bed, and, removing only her shoes, she crawled between the covers. Shivering in the cold bed, she longed for the warmth of Darren's arms, and wondered how he was spending the night.

Hours later, the wind calmed, and she got up to peer out the window. The snow seemed to have ceased, and, toward morning, she felt warmth stealing into the room, as the electric heaters chased away the cold.

Ginger tried to improve her tousled condition, but that was difficult when she didn't even have a comb. Her purse was still in the car. Considering that the first move was up to Darren, she sat down to wait. At about nine o'clock, he knocked on her door. She was more shy in his presence this morning than she'd been since the first few weeks of their acquaintance.

"Did you sleep any?" he asked.

She nodded. "Some." He didn't look as if he'd slept much, she thought, and she noted that expression of hopelessness which she hadn't seen in his eyes for a long time.

"I've been checking with the highway patrol. Now that the snow has stopped, the plows are out. In another hour we should be able to go on. Only about four inches of snow fell, and it didn't drift much after the wind stopped about midnight."

"Are you afraid to try the roads now?"

"No, and I have to get back to Lincoln. There's a restaurant about a mile east of here. We can eat breakfast there and get started. It will be slow traveling, but I'll be careful."

Darren was different during the trip to Lincoln. He had to devote his attention to driving, because the traffic often was confined to one-way passage, and he talked very little. When he did speak to her, she noted a tone in his voice which she hadn't heard before.

Should she apologize for what she'd said last night? More than once during her sleepless hours she had wished she'd guarded her speech. But would she have halted him in his purpose otherwise? She felt helpless to deal with him, especially when she loved him as she did.

When they arrived at her home, he drew her toward him and buried his face in her hair.

"You have the most beautiful hair I've ever seen on a woman. Have I ever told you that?"

"No," she whispered.

"That's another one of the things I've left unsaid too long." He released her and leaned his head back on the car's seat. "Ginger, I didn't sleep much last night, and I had plenty of time to think about what you said to me. You're right. I'm not fit company for you, and I've known it all along, but I just couldn't stay away from you. When I'm with you, I have a peace that I've never felt before in my life. But, as usual, I've been selfish, thinking of myself rather than of you."

"I'm sorry I said it," she said remorsefully.

"Don't be. You can't think any worse of me than I think of myself. I'm not trying to excuse my actions last night, but, if I hadn't been so exhausted, it wouldn't have happened. I wasn't thinking clearly. I hadn't slept for twenty-four hours, and I should have stayed in Lincoln and let you and Ken go on as you'd planned."

"It's all right. Let's forget it."

But he shook his head. "I've tried to be the kind of man you want me to be, Miss Prude, but I don't want to ruin your life; and I will ruin it, if I don't stay away from you. I know myself better than you do, and I'll take you one of these days whether you want me to or not. If I hadn't been trying to keep my promise to you, I would have tried something long ago. So, you're free, Ginger."

"It's too late now," she said.

"You're young, and you'll soon forget me if I leave you alone. Stay with Ken; he's more your type. But I want you to promise me something. Don't leave the bank and Lincoln because of me. You have a good job, your church is here, and it's convenient for you to go to school. I won't bother you again, but stay where I'll know how you're getting along. I'll worry about you if you go away."

Ginger's eyelids were stinging, and she felt tears ready to spill over the surface. *I can't live without him, and he's leaving me. I never should have told him that I loved him.* Her throat was too tight to utter a sound.

"You said last night that you'd never forgive yourself if I forced you to do something against your principles," Darren continued. "Well, I wouldn't forgive myself if I caused you to lose your self-respect."

She lifted her hand in a pleading gesture, and he held it and kissed her fingers softly. "Sweetheart, I admire you more than any person I've ever known. The way you've been patient and loving with me, and everyone else, has taught me what God is like. You're my ideal of a Christian. You practice what you preach."

He smiled and his words told her at last what she had longed to hear, but it was too late now. "I finally realized last night why I've taken such an interest in you. You see, Miss Prude, *I love you, too.* I should have recognized it sooner, but I've never really been in love before."

170

The tears were flowing freely now, running down her cheeks, and dripping from her chin. She couldn't remove her gaze from his face. He reached up and wiped the tears away, and kissed her softly on the lips. "Good-bye, Ginger. It's been good knowing you. You've been good for me."

She groped blindly for the door handle. When she couldn't find it, he reached across and opened the door. She stood in the snow and, through her tears, watched him drive away for the last time. Not even when she'd lost her grandmother had Ginger Wilson experienced such a sense of loss.

Ginger didn't think she could bear to go to work on Monday, but, in the weeks that followed, Darren kept his promise. He spent a great deal of time away from the bank, but, each time he returned, he swept Ginger with an appraising glance, and that was all. Soon it was common knowledge that his relationship with Ginger had altered. She saw knowing looks on some faces, amusement on others, and in her friends' faces she noted concern and sympathy.

Ginger thought that she couldn't stand it, but she had to for a while. She continued to go to classes, but she made no plans for the next semester. When her mother sent an early Christmas card with a sizable check and another warm invitation to visit them in Saudi Arabia, Ginger laid it aside, thinking that might be a way out for her. She would wait until after the first of the year. If, by that time, she hadn't gotten used to being without him, she would leave. She hadn't *promised* Darren that she would stay, even though he had asked.

Sally had come over for coffee and cookies, and she

and Ginger sat around the table, with Patrick sleeping on the couch. Ginger valued her friendship—and she appreciated the effort that Sally had made to ease her sorrow in the past weeks—but Ginger didn't want to talk to anyone. She nibbled on a cookie, and tried to keep her mind on Sally's conversation, but, after a long silence, Sally asked, "How long has it been since Mr. Banning has been to see you?"

"Not since that day we went to Hastings," Ginger said quietly.

"Roger told me to leave you alone," Sally said, "and I don't mean to pry, but it might help you to talk. It worries me to see the way you look. You have dark circles under your eyes, and you're losing weight. I'm afraid you'll be sick if you don't stop grieving over him."

"I can't talk about it, Sally."

"Ken says you haven't registered for next semester's classes," Sally continued.

"That's true," she said slowly.

"Then you're planning to leave Lincoln?"

"I think I must. I can't rid him from my life as long as I stay here. It's like biting on a toothache and hoping that will ease the pain. I dream about him at night, and every waking minute he's on my mind. When I go to the store, I buy food that he likes just in case he comes by unexpectedly as he used to. Yesterday, when I put a plate on the table for him, I knew I couldn't keep torturing myself. I have to get away."

Sally reached across the table and took Ginger's hand, and her eyes overflowed with tears. "I'm sorry," she said. "I feared this would happen, Ginger, but, the way he pursued you, I don't know what else you could have done."

"Oh, but don't blame Darren," Ginger protested. "I

know people are saying he's dropped me like he has everyone else. That isn't true. He's always been honest with me, right from the first, for he told me he wouldn't marry me. If I was foolish enough to fall in love with him, I have no one to blame but myself. But I couldn't marry him even if he wanted me to. The difference in our values is just too great. It's an insurmountable problem."

"No problem is too big for God," Sally assured her.

"I know that, and I've prayed that God would change his outlook on the better way of life."

"Then God will answer that prayer," Sally said. "Just keep your faith."

Chapter Ten

Ginger had been in the bank only a few minutes when Tina telephoned from her office across the lobby. "Come over a minute, Ginger," she said.

Tina's look was compassionate when Ginger entered the room. "Close the door, dear," she said softly. Ginger leaned against the door feeling suffocated. Her knees seemed too weak to hold her. Had something happened to Darren? She couldn't find the words to ask, but she waited breathlessly.

"Did you know that Mr. Banning had a son?" Tina asked.

Much surprised, Ginger reluctantly murmured, "Yes."

"He died yesterday."

Ginger gasped, hands at her throat, trying to still her throbbing pulse.

"The news came here at the bank after the rest of you had gone for the day," Tina continued. "I telephoned Mr. Banning at his apartment, and he left immediately for Colorado. He asked me to tell *you*, but not to mention it to anyone else."

"And he has to face this alone! Oh, Tina, he doesn't have anyone! I should be with him...but, if he'd

174

wanted me, he would have contacted me, I suppose." She knew that, under the terms of their separation, he had no choice but to leave her behind, but surely he would know that she'd want to help when he was in trouble.

"Do you want to tell me about it, Ginger?"

"No, I won't betray his confidence." She closed her eyes, and sobbed, "I love him, Tina."

"I know you do," Tina said as she put her arms around Ginger. "I've come to respect Mr. Banning a great deal since I've worked closely with him. I realize there's a fine man below the hard surface he presents to the world."

"But he's also a sad man, and he puts forth the hard surface to hide his loneliness. Now, when he needs me the most, I've driven him away!"

All day Ginger followed Darren's actions in her mind. She saw him land at the Denver airport and make the long drive to the institution to claim the body of his son. She followed him to the old homestead, saw him stop in front of the house and relive his youth and blighted hopes. She saw the cemetery, and the open grave where the boy would be buried beside Rhonda. Would he weep, or would he stand in stunned silence as his last remaining relative was taken from him? As his wife, she could have accompanied him, shared his sorrow, and given him comfort. Would he know she was thinking about him, and praying for him?

November was almost gone when Darren returned to Lincoln, and Ginger was shocked at his appearance. His youthful vigor was lacking, and his unhappiness was more evident than ever. He looked tired and emaciated, as if he hadn't slept or eaten in weeks. What could she do? He hadn't spoken to her since that trip to Hastings several weeks ago. Would it hurt to voice her sympathy? She longed to help him, and she prayed for guidance.

The next morning, when she was eating breakfast, she noted that the date was November 27, and the importance of that date jarred her memory. Suddenly she was back at the ranch reading the family records in the Bible. *Today was Darren's birthday*. Could that give her an excuse to show her sympathy without reviving their old passions?

He was already at the bank when she arrived. Learning from Tina that he was alone, she slipped quietly into the office. He was sitting, head bowed in his hands, and he didn't hear her enter. She wanted to run to him and cradle him in her arms, but she remained by the door, her hands behind her back.

"I'm sorry, Darren," she said softly.

When he lifted his head, she looked away to avoid the agony in his eyes. "I know, Ginger," he said.

"I wish I could have been there, but my thoughts and prayers were with you all the time."

"I know that, too," he said with a pathetic smile that caused tears to sting Ginger's eyes. "I felt them, and it was almost the same as if you were with me. I wouldn't have made it, otherwise."

"Will you come for dinner tonight?"

A strange expression crossed his face. "Do you know that's the first time you've ever asked me to come to see you?"

She felt herself blushing. "You haven't needed me before."

"I've always needed you, Ginger, but I suppose I'm the 'stray dog' you're befriending now," he said glumly.

"I'd hardly consider you a 'stray dog.'"

He looked out the window for a few minutes. Thick clouds hung over the city, and the day seemed as gloomy as his face. "No, Ginger, I won't come. If I wasn't fit company before, I'm even less so now. I'm cold inside. I have no interest in anything. I don't even care if I make any more money."

"I'll be looking for you at six o'clock," she said softly. But, that evening, as she prepared some of his favorite food, her hands trembled at the fear that he would ignore her invitation. She planned to serve Swiss steak, mashed potatoes, buttered peas, and lettuce wedges with creamy French dressing. She didn't have time to make a birthday cake, but she did bake a peach cobbler which she could serve warm with thick cream.

"He did come," she said aloud when she heard the Cadillac drive into its accustomed place. But the moment was awkward for them when he entered the living room. They looked at each other silently for a few minutes, and then his gaze moved around the room. Ginger knew how unfavorably her cramped living quarters compared with his home, but, as he looked at her small kitchen and living area, a fondness came into his eyes which he couldn't conceal.

"I've missed being here, Ginger," he said slowly.

She locked her hands behind her back to keep from touching him. Then she busied herself with the final meal preparations. Handing him a cup of coffee, she said, "Sit down for a minute, Darren. I'll be ready as soon as I mash the potatoes."

He ate heartily, and she had the feeling that he hadn't eaten much since his son's death. They didn't talk a great deal, for they'd passed the point where conversation was necessary. Togetherness was the

177

healing antidote he needed.

"Do you want me to help with the dishes, Ginger?" he asked.

"No, it won't take me long. Why don't you rest?"

He lay down on the couch, and was soon asleep. He slept long after she'd finished her work. Before he awakened, Ginger placed two wrapped packages on the table beside him. Then she got out her sewing and sat quietly.

After he awakened, he watched her for a time before he pushed some cushions behind his back, and moved to a reclining position on the couch. "What are you doing now, Miss Prude?"

"Hemming a wool skirt I made last week."

"Is that the material I brought you from Canada?"

Blushing a little, she admitted, "Yes, and I have enough left to make a coat when I get the time."

He noticed the packages on the table, and she said, "Happy birthday, Darren."

He asked in surprise, "What is today?" He hadn't even remembered his birthday!

"November 27."

"But how did you know?"

"I saw it in the family Bible last summer at the ranch."

"I'm thirty-six years old, Ginger, and it seems that I've lived a lifetime in the past two weeks." He started talking then, and Ginger listened without comment. For hours he talked, and she didn't think that he left out a single event in his whole life. She heard about his boyhood and the poverty on the farm, the difficult years of working his way through school, and the time when he had started to prosper—when everything he'd touched had turned to money.

At last, in graphic detail, he recounted the death of

178

the boy. "I had wanted him dead, Ginger; I don't mind telling you that. But, when it happened, I felt guilty, as if there were something more I could have done for him."

"Don't feel guilty, Darren. Since I was out there with you last summer, I've studied about his disability. Such children rarely live to be adults. There wasn't anything else you could have done. And I'm telling you the truth—you should take *no* responsibility for the child's affliction. You'd done nothing to cause it."

"But you know the Bible speaks of the sins of the fathers being visited on their children."

Smiling, she said, "I doubt that, at nineteen, you had committed such terrible sins, and, regardless, in the New Testament, when Jesus was asked whose sin had caused a man's blindness, he said it wasn't his sin *or* his parents'. The best of people, or the worst, have problems like this. I tell you, you should quit blaming yourself."

"I hope so, Ginger." He sat up and looked at the packages. "I hardly know how to act. No one has ever given me gifts except my mother." The comment saddened Ginger. Despite his millions, he possessed so little love and devotion.

Ginger remembered the fit she'd thrown when he had wanted to give her the emerald necklace for her birthday, but, if he had thought of it, he said nothing.

He opened the big gift first, and smiled with pleasure when he saw the white sweater with the golden triangle decoration on the pocket. "Did you make it yourself?" At her nod, he added, "You're very talented, Ginger."

He tried on the sweater, and the fit was perfect. His handsome face seemed to lose some of the lines of fatigue as he admired the gift. With his dark skin and

179

hair, white was an attractive shade for his clothes.

Possibly he guessed the content of the smaller package, for he held it a bit before opening it. The New Testament seemed out of place in his hand, but she said pleadingly, "Please read it, Darren. You'll find comfort and the answer to your need there. I'm praying that you will."

"I'll try, Miss Prude, but I'm afraid I'm a lost cause."

He left without touching her, but he dropped a fatherly peck on her forehead. Somehow Ginger was more confident than ever before that she was about to see the fulfillment of God's promise, "All things work together for good to them that love God."

Silent night! Holy night!
Guiding star, lend thy light!
See the Eastern wise men bring
Gifts and homage to our King!
Christ the Savior is born,
Christ the Savior is born.

The words of the familiar song faded into the night as the carolers moved from one mobile home to another. Ginger covered her ears to blot out the sound which, at one time, would have made her happy, but not tonight. A year ago, her grandmother was still living. Now she had lost her—and Darren, too—and tears filled her eyes. Christmas was only a few days away, and she thought that she couldn't bear the holiday festivities in her present state of mind.

Once, Ginger picked up the phone receiver, and started to dial Darren's number. She wanted to say, "Come back to me, and I'll take you on any conditions," but her morals were stronger than her heart, and she didn't complete the call.

She huddled on the couch, and finally dozed for a few minutes. She was awakened by the ringing of the doorbell. When she opened the door, Darren entered diffidently. For a moment, she thought that she must be dreaming, but a cold blast of wind, swirling snow-flakes into the room, made her realize that it was all real enough.

Darren took off his coat and laid a roll of paper on the counter top before he spoke. "Ginger, I've loved you since that day you stood by the highway with the wind blowing your hair every-which-way, and I've learned in these weeks we've been separated that nothing I have means anything to me if I've lost you. I don't want to live without you, sweetheart."

Ginger's heart was pounding until it almost choked her. Her thoughts were in a turmoil, but she didn't hesitate when he held out his arms to her. He hugged her to him until she could hardly breathe, but she managed to whisper, "I can live without you, Darren, but it isn't much fun." She raised her lips to his. When he released her, he sat in the rocking chair and drew her onto his lap.

"I've come to some decisions the past few days that will affect my life as well as yours. Since you gave that Testament to me, I've read it. Although I didn't under-stand many of the words, one place I read said some-thing about the rich of the world shouldn't set their hopes on riches, or something like that. Do you know what I mean?"

Ginger reached for her Bible lying on the table. She opened it to 1 Timothy 6:17. "Charge them that are rich in this world, that they be not highminded, nor trust in uncertain riches, but in the living God, who giveth us richly all things to enjoy," she read aloud.

"That's it. Those words must have been written es-

181

pecially for me. I'm ashamed of the way I thought that I had more power than God, but I'm changing. And it isn't just to get you. It's more than that, because I can't have any peace within myself as long as I make possessions my greatest priority. I realize that now, and, even if you send me away tonight, I'll never be the way I used to be."

"Oh, my darling," she whispered, "I've never loved you more."

Her arms went around his neck, as if she never intended to let him go again, and she almost didn't. She kept pulling his head down again and again to kiss him until Darren finally broke their embrace.

"Will you behave?" he said in mock severity. "I'm happy, too, but I told you I wanted to *talk* tonight. I have some things to tell you. But first, will you spend Christmas with me at the ranch? I'll warn you that Melissa and Ike won't be there."

Her joy faded a little. "I'll have to work," she said.

"You don't have a job, if you're referring to Midland Bank. I've fired you."

"Don't tease me," she murmured with downcast eyes.

"Who's teasing? I tell you we no longer need your services at Midland Bank." He took a box from his pocket. "I have another job in mind for you. Will you go to the ranch with me, if you have these on your finger?" He opened the box, and a huge diamond solitaire glittered at her. But her eyes scarcely noticed it, as she saw the wide wedding band, where dozens of miniature diamonds formed the initials "GWB."

"Ginger Wilson Banning?" she whispered in awe. "Do you mean it, Darren?"

The telephone rang, and Ginger jumped from his

lap, muttering, "We should have taken that off the hook!"

"Ginger," Mrs. Gainer's voice sounded throughout the room. "I notice that Mr. Banning is at your home. Just a few hours ago, I received by special messenger a check from him for $25,000. Ask him if there's some mistake."

Ginger turned wondering eyes toward Darren, who winked at her and said, "Tell her to accept it with my compliments."

When she hung up the receiver, Ginger stared at him in amazement, and watched as he took a blueprint from the cardboard tube he'd brought with him.

He spread the blueprint on the bar, explaining that it was for a six-dwelling apartment complex complete with inner court containing a swimming pool and play area. "I let the contract on this yesterday, and construction will start in the spring for the ranch workers and their families."

Ginger was still speechless, but, when he sat down in a chair, she knelt by his side and clasped her arms around his knees. "Tell me more, Darren," she whispered, pride and respect for him evident in her eyes.

"There isn't much more to tell, except that I've endowed the institution where my son lived. The endowment will serve as a perpetual memorial to him."

Love shone from tearful eyes as she said, "Now you're that big man I've wanted you to be! You'll never be able to outgive God, darling. He's going to lead you on to better and greater things."

He pulled her to his lap again. "I don't know what kind of magic you used, Miss Prude, but you've gotten everything you wanted, haven't you?"

"Yes, including you," she said archly.

"Then you'll agree to become Mrs. Darren Banning?"

"As soon as possible," she assured him without hesitation.

"That will be Wednesday. If we get the license tomorrow, we can be married the morning of Christmas Eve, and be at the ranch that night. And now that I've given away a fortune, will you let me spend some money on you?"

"Whatever you say," she told him. "From now on, you're the head of the family, and I'll do what you tell me."

He looked at her skeptically. "I doubt that, but, at any rate, I'm not expecting such docility. You'll still have to keep me in line, for I won't become perfect overnight. And I'm depending on you to contribute all the common sense needed to rear our children."

"Children!" Ginger gasped. "Have you gotten over your fear about that?"

"No, not completely, but I've decided to trust that to God, too."

Ginger's joy beamed from her face. "Oh, I do *want* to give you a child, Darren." She was breathless in her excitement. "I don't think I can stand anymore happiness."

"You haven't heard anything yet. Wait until I tell you what we're going to do for the next month."

He lifted her to her feet and moved to the couch. She cuddled close to him, and clasped her arms around his middle.

"First, I meant that you weren't going back to the bank. They'll have to get along without you until they can hire someone else. We'll arrange for the license and make plans for our marriage in the morning, and you can have the kind of wedding you want. If you

184

prefer only Roger and Sally with us, fine, but, if you'd like a big ceremony with all the frills, I'll pay for it.

"We're also going shopping for your wedding dress and a complete trousseau. You're not to look at the prices; only choose exactly what you want. I'm giving you a beautiful wedding and honeymoon. Okay?"

She nodded, and her eyes were shining.

"As soon as we're married we'll go to the ranch. Ike and Melissa will be gone. I'm going to lock the door, take the phone off the hook, and shoot anyone who sets foot on the premises. When I've proven to you how much I love you, and how serious I am about this husband business, I might bring you back to civilization. What do you think of that?"

"Is that a promise?" she murmured as she nibbled softly on his ear.

"The trousseau isn't for the ranch, for I'm not particular about what you wear up there. But, soon after the first of the year, we're taking a trip. I want you dressed to perfection then."

"Where are we going?"

He took an airline itinerary from his pocket. "How does this sound?" She looked at the paper as he read aloud, "London, Paris, Nice, Rome, Athens, Tel Aviv, Alexandria, and Saudi Arabia."

"Saudi Arabia!" she cried. "Are we going to see my mother?"

"Yes. I have some business interests in the Middle East, but mainly we're going to see her."

"You'll spoil me," Ginger said, "but I'll never stop loving you. I've been so unhappy these weeks when I thought I'd lost you. Now you've made me happier than I've ever been."

His arms clasped her tightly, and he kissed her until Ginger lay limp in his embrace. Her whole body strained with emotion, leading her on to that moment when she would experience the fullness of his love for her.

Darren put her away regretfully, and said, "I'm leaving now, sweetheart, but, two nights from now, I'll be staying."

"I know that. I've no intention of letting you leave then, or ever again."

Ginger watched him leave, and, for the first time, she didn't question his return. He was hers for a lifetime.

Dear Reader:

I am committed to bringing you the kind of romantic novels you want to read. Please fill out the brief questionnaire below so we will know what you like most in Cherish Romances™.

Mail to: Etta Wilson
Thomas Nelson Publishers
P.O. Box 141000
Nashville, Tenn. 37214

1. Why did you buy this Cherish Romance™?

   ☐ Author
   ☐ Back cover description
   ☐ Christian story
   ☐ Cover art

   ☐ Recommendation from others
   ☐ Title
   ☐ Other_____

2. What did you like best about this book?

   ☐ Heroine
   ☐ Hero
   ☐ Christian elements

   ☐ Setting
   ☐ Story Line
   ☐ Secondary characters

3. Where did you buy this book?

   ☐ Christian bookstore
   ☐ Supermarket
   ☐ Drugstore

   ☐ General bookstore
   ☐ Book Club
   ☐ Other (specify)_____

4. Are you interested in buying other Cherish Ro-
   mances~TM~?

   ☐ Very interested   ☐ Somewhat interested
                    ☐ Not interested

5. Please indicate your age group.
   ☐ Under 18   ☐ 25-34
   ☐ 18-24   ☐ 35-49   ☐ Over 50

6. Comments or suggestions?

7. Would you like to receive a free copy of the Cherish
Romance~TM~ newsletter? If so, please fill in your name
and address.

Name _____

Address _____

City _____ State _____ Zip _____

7352-8